TEXAS FURY

Jim Hatfield rode into a land where outlaws ran roughshod and lawmen laid low. He found a gang drunk with power running guns and stealing silver. He found himself in an ambush of cold steel and burning death. But Texas Rangers don't scare easy. When the outlaws came gunning for the bloody showdown, Jim answered them the Texas way—and made it stick with hot lead!

Leslie Scott was born in Lewisburg, West Virginia. During the Great War, he joined the French Foreign Legion and spent four years in the trenches. In the 1920s he worked as a mining engineer and bridge builder in the western American states and in China before settling in New York. A bar-room discussion in 1934 with Leo Margulies, who was managing editor for Standard Magazines, prompted Scott to try writing fiction. He went on to create two of the most notable series characters in Western pulp magazines. In 1936, Standard Magazines launched, and in *Texas Rangers*, Scott under the house name of Jackson Cole created Jim Hatfield, Texas Ranger, a character whose popularity was so great with readers that this magazine featuring his adventures lasted until 1958. When others eventually began contributing Jim Hatfield stories, Scott created another Texas Ranger hero, Walt Slade, better known as *El Halcon*, the Hawk, whose exploits were regularly featured in *Thrilling Western*. In the 1950s Scott moved quickly into writing book-length adventures about both Jim Hatfield and Walt Slade in long series of original paperback Westerns. At the same time, however, Scott was also doing some of his best work in hardcover Westerns published by Arcadia House; thoughtful, well-constructed stories, with engaging characters and authentic settings and situations. Among the best of these, surely, are *Silver City* (1953), *Longhorn Empire* (1954), *The Trail Builders* (1956), and *Blood on the Rio Grande* (1959). In these hardcover Westerns, many of which have never been reprinted, Scott proved himself highly capable of writing traditional Western stories with characters who have sufficient depth to change in the course of the narrative and with a degree of authenticity and historical accuracy absent from many of his series stories.

TEXAS FURY

Jackson Cole

GUNSMOKE

This hardback edition 2005
by BBC Audiobooks Ltd
by arrangement with
Golden West Literary Agency

ISBN 1 4056 8044 X

British Library Cataloguing in Publication Data available.

Printed and bound in Great Britain by
Antony Rowe Ltd., Chippenham, Wiltshire

1

HOLD IT, Goldy! What the blazes is going on around that bend?"

Jim Hatfield jerked his tall golden sorrel to a halt as a crackle of gun fire sounded beyond where the brush flanked trail curved sharply out of sight. As he peered at the bristle of growth that hid the continuation of the track, there came a solid and conclusive thump and an exultant whoop. The whoop was followed almost instantly by a volley of unearthly yells and a frantic drumming of horses' irons.

Around the curve bulged three horsemen, waving their arms, beating themselves with their hats, howling curses. From the saddle horn of the rearmost rider stretched a rope, and at the end of the rope bumped and bounded a dome-shaped object. The horsemen straightened out on the trail, going like the devil beating tanbark.

Skating around the bend as if blown by the wind, came a stocky old man, his gray whiskers fanning out over his shoulders. He brandished a double-barrelled shotgun. He halted, his boots kicking up puffs of dust, clamped the butt of the shotgun against his shoulder and threw down with deadly aim. The rearmost rider, at the moment, was leaning far forward on his horse's neck, slapping at his back and shoulders.

The shotgun let go with a deafening double roar and a

cloud of smoke. The rearmost rider screeched like a lost soul and shot straight up in his stirrups, clapping both hands to a certain humble portion of his frame. He twisted around, half reached for his Colt; but as the old-ster threw open the breech of his scattergun, he shot for-ward again, rearing high out of his saddle, and rode for his life.

As Hatfield stared in amazement, the foremost horse-man let out a bellow of warning,

"Hightail, cowboy, or they'll get you, too!" he bawled, thrashing about with both arms. "Inter the brush, if yuh value yore hide!"

Hatfield peered with outthrust neck, then whirled Goldy "on a dime" and led the procession into the brush. For several hundred yards he rode at a mad gallop, swerving around trunks, bending under low branches, crackling through thorns and twigs. Behind him crashed the wild-eyed trio of cowboys, still slapping and waving and volleying curses. Finally, in the shade of a tall bush, Hatfield pulled Goldy to a blowing halt and waited for the others to catch up. A moment later they slithered to a standstill beside him.

"Did yuh ever hear of anythin' so blankety-blank loco?" the foremost, a beefy-faced individual with fierce side whiskers, appealed to Hatfield. "Droppin' a loop on a beehive! I'm speckled as a turkey egg!"

The rearmost rider, who still stood stiffly erect in his stirrups, let out an injured howl.

"You and yore speckles!" he yelped. "That blankety-blank old pelican lined me dead center with both barrels of that scattergun! And me wearin' nothin' but a pair of thin overalls!"

"I wish he'd used buckshot on yuh!" the other declared vindictively. "Ropin' a beehive!"

Hatfield gazed at the trio with mirthful eyes.

"Reckon he'll know better next time," he predicted.

"Bees are hard to run a brand on. Understand there's quite a few of 'em in this section."

"That's right," agreed the beefy-faced man. "Money in bees, for folks what know how to handle 'em. Hafta move the hives about, though, as they work out the flowers around."

"I moved one," grunted the standing gent, feeling gingerly behind him.

"Uh-huh, and it moved you!" growled the beefy-faced man. He turned his gaze back to Hatfield.

"I'm Clem Shore," he announced. "The fuzzy brained horned toad with the bird shot holes in his pants is Bert Pierce. The gent hidin' behind the nose is Beak Prescott. We ride for the Tumblin' K, over to the northeast of here. We *were* figgerin' to go home."

"How we goin' to do it?" wailed the big-nosed Prescott, after Hatfield had supplied his name and they had gravely shaken hands. "That old hellion is liable to be prowlin' around out here with his scattergun. I got bee stings enough, without a dose of lead pizenin'."

All three glanced apprehensively in the direction of the trail.

"The branch-off to our spread is just around the bend," Shore explained. "We was just aimin' to turn off when Bert got that loco notion of droppin' a loop on the beehive. We didn't have time for no turnin' after that. We gotta pass old Andy Cahil's place to get to the fork." He ran a speculative glance over Hatfield's much more than six feet of broad shouldered, lean-wasted height.

"Say, feller," he insinuated, "you weren't mixed up in the shindig. Suppose yuh mosey out and make peace pow-wow with the old pelican. Mebbe yuh can gab him into lettin' us ride past without stoppin' lead."

"Well, it has the appearance of a hefty chore," Hatfield returned meditatively, "pertickler if those bees are still mavericking around."

He held up his hand. The others cocked their ears. From beyond the brush came a tinny banging, as if someone were industriously beating a wash basin with a club.

"That's better," he said. "He's trying to get 'em to swarm. I've a notion he'll be riding herd on 'em in a mite and corralling 'em back in the hive. Reckon I can take a chance. You jiggers stay out of sight around the bend till I give the word."

Leaving the Tumbling K punchers peering apprehensively from the straggle of brush along the trail, Hatfield rode around the bend at a leisurely pace but keeping a sharp lookout for the winged enemy. As he rounded the curve, the growth fell away on the left-hand side, leaving a wide clearing. A sturdily built cabin sat some distance from the trail and at the edge of a cultivated patch of ground. On the flat space before the cabin were some two dozen or more of the dome-shaped hives. Beside one stood the old man, industriously beating a tin tub with a stick. About him buzzed and swirled the bees. A steady trickle disappeared into the hole at the base of the hive.

The oldster glanced up quickly at the sound of Goldy's irons and turned toward his shotgun, that leaned conveniently against the hive. Then, seeing that the advancing horseman was not one of the turbulent trio of pranksters, he waved the club in a gesture of invitation.

"Just take it easy and they won't bother yuh," he said, apropos of the disturbed honey gatherers. "What became of them three horned toads what follered yuh inter the brush? I hope they busted their dadblamed necks. They stampeded my bees. Won't be any good the rest of the afternoon."

Hatfield chuckled. "They're still holed up in the bushes," he said. "They want to come out and go home."

"Let 'em scratch their way through the mesquite," the oldster grunted.

"I figger they got a bellyful," Hatfield smiled. "The one who looped the hive is standing in his stirrups and the other two look plumb sorrowful."

Old Andy Cahil still glowered, but he was cooling visibly. He permitted himself a creaky chuckle.

"Reckon I peppered that lanky Bert Pierce proper," he said. "I'm purty ac'rate with old Betsy there," he added, with a contemplative glance at the shotgun. "Reckon they won't bother my bees soon again. They ain't bad young fellers—just full of the Old Harry."

A plaintive call sounded from beyond the bend—

"How yuh comin' on, feller?"

"Reckon it's safe to show," Hatfield called back.

A moment later the trio sidled around the curve, glancing slantwise and somewhat apprehensively at the elderly bee owner.

"We won't do it again, Uncle Andy," said the red-faced Shore. "Reckon we made a mistake."

"From the looks of yuh, I'd say yuh did," old Andy returned, eyeing their swollen faces and the stiffly upright posture of Pierce with grim satisfaction."

"I'd rather try to head a herd of stampedin' longhorns than get into a rukus with a bunch of them winged scorpions of yours," declared Shore. "And Bert ain't gonna eat comfortable, 'cept from the mantlepiece, for a week. We're plumb ready to call it quits and head for home."

He glanced toward where a fork of the trail rambled off across the prairie to the east, veering slightly in a northerly direction.

"Get goin', then," grunted Cahil. He resumed the beating of his tub to entice the remaining bees into the hive. Shore turned to Hatfield.

"Feller, yuh give us a big lift," he said. "How about amblin' over to the spread for a s'roundin'? We got a good cook."

Hatfield hesitated a moment. "Was figgering on making that town of Cibolero, to the north of here, before
dark," he said.

"Yuh can't never do it," Shore said. "It's nigh onto fifteen miles, and the sun's nearly set already. Come on over
to the Tumblin' K and spend the night. The bunkhouse
is filled up, but there's spare rooms in the Bull's Mansh,
and the Old Man's a sociable cuss. Yuh'll like him. He's
not quite as tall but purty nigh as broad as you are, and
a slight thicker around the middle. Likes to eat, so the
chuck is always prime."

"Sounds good," Hatfield admitted. "I've almost forgot-
ten how to swallow, and I reckon my cayuse could do
with something besides grass for a change."

"Ridin' the chuck line is hard on the belly in a section
like this," Shore agreed. "That's some horse yuh got, all
right, feller."

"Old Goldy will do," Hatfield admitted.

"Let's get goin'," Pierce interrupted plaintively. "I'm
gettin' almighty tired of standin' up. I craves a cushion."

Saying goodbye to Andy Cahil, they turned into the
side track, rode for perhaps a quarter of a mile through
thick growth and reached the open rangeland.

"Half an hour and we'll sight the *casa*," said Shore.
"Sets close to the hills over there to the east."

The hills in question, diagonalling out of the northeast,
swept southward then west in a splendid curve. They in-
creased in height as they veered to the west, their summits rugged and craggy. Beyond them, Hatfield knew,
was an expanse of desert that rolled on to the gorge of
the Rio Grande and the Carmen Mountains of Mexico.

As they drew nearer the brown and swelling masses,
Hatfield noted that, far up the slope, a trail clung to
the precipitous side of the sage, following the contours,
winding southward, a gray and dusty streak, till it

writhed wearily up the towering southern wall and vanished through a notch in its crest.

Shore noticed the direction of his gaze. "That's the old Smugglers' Trail," he remarked. "She was a lively one in the old days. The oilers hauled dobe dollars and dope and Chinamen inter Texas over it, and took back goods the Custom House gents never got a look at. Many a herd rolled over that track, too. Folks say that more'n one big cattleman of this section got his start runnin' wet cows across the Rio and north by way of the Smuggler. Then, later on, other gents with loose business notions run calves them critters was the granddaddys of south inter *manana* land and a market where brands didn't count over much. Uh-huh, she was lively in the old days."

"She ain't so dull nowadays," Beak Prescott grunted. "A lot of cows have showed up missin' in this section of late, and if they don't go south by way of the Smuggler, how do they go?"

"Other things been missin', too," put in Pierce. "That strongbox with the Monarch Mine payroll in it didn't go straight up in the air when it got lifted off the Cibolero stage. And the railroad is sort of interested in gents that ride the Smuggler since the Sunrise Flyer got piled up and the express car blowed."

The others nodded solemnly. Hatfield looked thoughtful, but said nothing.

A little later they rounded a final clump of thicket and the Tumbling K ranchhouse came into view, its peaked roof projecting above the wide tops of the grove of oaks that surrounded it. Hatfield noted the commodious bunkhouse, set rather far behind the *casa*, the tight corral, roomy barns and other well cared for outbuildings.

A wrangler took their horses and led them to the barn. Hatfield was ushered into the big main living room of the ranchhouse and introduced to old Caswell Klingman, the Tumbling K owner.

Hatfield, who missed nothing of what surrounded him, noted that the room was comfortably furnished and with considerable taste. There were paintings on the wall, a well stocked bookcase, commodious chairs. In one corner stood a massive iron safe, its door closed. After a swift, all-embracing glance, he turned his attention to his host.

Klingman was a tall, bulky and broad-shouldered man of between fifty and sixty. He had kindly, twinkling blue eyes, a luxuriant beard that rippled down over his chest and a firm but humorous mouth. He shook hands cordially. He was considerably more than six feet in height, but just the same he had to raise his gaze somewhat to meet the long, level green eyes of the man a stern old Lieutenant of Rangers had named The Lone Wolf.

"Just in time to eat," he said. "Cook's puttin' chuck on the table right now. I hear the boys washin' up out back. Get the dust off yuh, son, and make ready to set."

Hatfield enjoyed an excellent dinner in the company of Klingman and the dozen Tumbling K riders. They were a jovial lot of young hellions who roared with laughter over the bee roping and its results. A cushion was provided for Bert Pierce; Klingman promised needed surgical attention after supper.

"You fellers had better try and get them bee stingers out of yuh, too," he advised. "They fester sometimes if they ain't taken out. And keep away from that old bee herder after this. Next time he's liable to use buckshot on yuh. Lucky he wasn't packin' that old Sharpes Buffalo gun or some of yuh might not be here to tell about it. Old Andy is bad medicine when he gets riled."

"Yuh don't need to tell me that, Boss," observed Pierce, moving tenderly on his cushion.

After a gabfest in the living room, Hatfield was shown to the second floor where he would sleep.

"I bed down in the first room in this end of the hall," Klingman observed, as he led the way up the stairs from

the living room. "You take the next one. The others are
vacant and closed up. The boys used to spread their rolls
in 'em, but when I spread out and took on more hands, I
had to build the bunkhouse and the jiggers like to herd
together, so there's nobody left in the house but me.
Hammer on the wall if yuh happen to want anythin'
durin' the night."

"Don't figger to open my eyes before daylight, once I
close them," Hatfield replied. "Riding all last night."

Klingman shot him a keen glance, but in keeping with
western custom, forbore asking questions. He opened the
door to the room Hatfield would occupy, indicated the
lamp on the table and said goodnight.

Hatfield closed the door and glanced about. Moonlight
streamed in through the open window, revealing a comfortable bed, chairs and other furnishings. Neglecting the
lamp, he crossed to the window and glanced out. Then,
instead of at once going to bed, he drew a chair to the
window and sat down, leaning his arms on the ledge and
resting his chin upon them.

For some time he sat watching the moonlight make
fantastic patterns on the ground as the tree branches
swayed gently in a faint wind, and thinking deeply.
Through an opening in the foliage he could see the swelling bulk of the hills to the east, with the winding ribbon
of the Smugglers' Trail standing out like a gray scar
against the moon silvered background. Through the
opening, perhaps a score of yards of the trail was visible,
little more than a thin line in the distance and the decep-
tive moonlight. His gaze centered on it as he thought
over the reasons for his coming to this isolated rincon of
the Big Bend country. His black brows drew together
until the furrow of concentration was deep between
them. He seemed to hear the rumbling voice of old Captain Bill McDowell at Ranger headquarters—

"The Customs authorities admit they're licked. They're

runnin' around in circles tryin' to figger what it's all about. Stuff comin' through from the South, loads of it, but, so far as they can find out, nothin' goin' back to *manana* land from the North. Of course, the smugglers may be takin' their pay in spot cash, but if they are, it's a most unusual procedure. They can do a heap better by takin' their returns in goods that sell high down in *Mejico* or can be slipped out the ports to foreign markets. That's the pattern they most always follow. This time they're not doin' it. As I pointed out to the Customs official, the Rangers aren't particularly interested in violation of the revenue laws; but, as he pointed out, crimes of violence, in connection with their shenanigans, have been committed on Texas soil. That makes it a horse with a different brand. So I reckon it's up to us to lend 'em a hand. Anythin' to go on? Not a dadblamed thing. Yuh're strictly on yore own and startin' from the end of the trail; but that isn't overly unusual for the Lone Wolf. *Adios*, Jim, and clear ridin'!"

Hatfield chuckled as he recalled the old Ranger Captain's laconic dismissal. He continued to stare at the narrow ribbon of trail, without really seeing it. Abruptly, however, he leaned forward, his eyes narrowing slightly, his attention intensely focused on the wavering gray line that clung to the brown hillside.

Into his range of vision, as if drawn by an invisible string, a speeding horseman had flickered. After the first came others, until Hatfield had counted a full dozen. Silent misty, vague and unreal in the moonlight, they flashed past like pictures on a screen. As ghosts they came, as ghosts they vanished, bursting from the shadow to the south, merging with the shadow to the north. No click of hoof or jingle of bridle irons came to his ears, no word of casual conversation. Spectres of the silent night, for a moment they *were*, then they were not.

Hatfield stared at the empty thread of trail, half believing that he had been the victim of an hallucination. Then he shook his black head. No, it was no phantom of the moonlight he had seen. The speeding horsemen had been flesh and blood riders heading northward at a swift pace. Of course, he realized, the incident could have been nothing more unusual than an outfit of cowboys heading for town; but he had a feeling that what he had seen was no troop of skylarking waddies out for a mite of diversion. There had been a trace of set purpose about the hard riding vision of the night that was disquieting. Well, there was nothing he could do about it at the moment. But he had an uneasy premonition that he would hear more, and something not pleasant, relative to the ghostly troop. He slouched forward again, still thinking, and at the same time trying to get up enough energy to undress and go to bed. Before he could rouse his tired body sufficiently to do so, his head drooped still more, his eyelids closed, and he slept.

2

MANY MILES north of where Jim Hatfield slept the sleep of exhaustion, his head pillowed on his forearms, a big old man sat before a blazing fireplace and dreamed a splendid dream. In the flickering flames he saw pictures —pictures of a mighty host surging southward across the purple mountains of Mexico. He saw the armed might of the tyrannical forces of *El Presidente* melt before their flaming rifles, fled headlong and vanish. On and on, across wide plains, through mountain passes, where the white streak of the *gave* foamed a thousand feet below, over rushing rivers, through the desert sands, thundering ever southward, their goal a city set in a valley that swings like a suspension bridge in the clouds between its mountain piers. Ahead, two towering volcanoes soared into the southern sky. His charger's hoofs thundered on streets that were old when the mailed feet of the iron men of Spain clashed upon their stones. He saw the Castle of Chapultepec on its crag, the vast cathedral flinging its spires into the blue. He entered the *Palacio Nacional* and watched a strikingly tall and imposing figure raise a hand to take the oath of office, while his crusading soldiers stood at attention and guns thundered a salute.

A smile played across the craggy features of the old dreamer as he visualized a united Mexico no longer torn by strife and hampered by dissension—prosperous,

14

powerful, progressive, with her peoples' will her only law from the Great River on the north to the blue mountain wall on the south—a mighty nation of peace and plenty, the grand creation of his own brain and hand.

He stood up, towering in his broad-shouldered, deep-chested might, the firelight gleaming on the lion's mane of iron-gray hair that swept back grandly from his big dome-shaped forehead. He stretched his long arms above his head, his powerful fingers reaching toward the beamed ceiling of the lofty room. He turned sharply at the sound of hoofbeats on the roadway that wound up from the trail to his spacious ranchhouse. The hoofbeats ceased. There was a jingle of bridle irons and a creaking of saddle leather.

"Okay, Captain Ben? It's Mort!" a voice called.

The old man crossed quickly to the door, the swing of his stride and the elasticity of his step showing he had not yet lost the fire of his youth, and flung the door open.

"Come on in," he shouted in deep, musical tones.

There was a clumping of boots on the steps, the veranda boards creaked and a squat, powerfully built man loomed in the lamplight. He strode into the room, glancing keenly about from under his low drawn hat-brim. In his wake, ten or eleven men filed into the room. The old man closed the door, gestured to chairs and a long couch. The visitors seated themselves, cuffed off their hats and eyed their host.

They were bronzed, muscular men with a healthy out-door look about them. Diverse as to build, size and feature, they had one thing in common, an alert watchfulness to their eyes. The man called Mort had a hard, straight mouth, a prominent nose and a jutting chin. When he spoke, his lips moved not at all.

"We made delivery," he said without preamble. "A big shipment, too. Tomorrow night we collect the goods and run 'em back south. Okay?"

"Good!" the other applauded. "And how about recruits?"

"A hundred, and a little over, new ones herded in," Mort replied. "Sancho is larrupin' them into shape."

"Good," the other repeated. "Sancho is a fine man—capable, loyal. Get him more to work with."

Mort's thin lips twitched slightly, his watchful eyes gleamed, as if with cynical amusement. The others stared ahead of them with wooden expressions.

The old man procured bottles and glasses from a cupboard. Drinks were downed. There was a little desultory conversation about nothing in particular. Then Mort stood up, sucking the drops of the whiskey from his drooping mustache.

"Reckon we'll be ridin'," he remarked.

"Good idea," the old man nodded, "you should be back across the River before daylight, if possible. No sense in anything that might lead to trouble right now. Things are going smoothly, and we want to keep them that way. Keep yore eyes open, too; there's a bad bunch operatin' in this section. Wouldn't want yuh to run into them and end up in a shindig. Nothin' gained by such rukuses."

Again Mort's lips twitched. "Yuh're right," he agreed. "Reckon we could handle anythin' we run up against, but there ain't no sense in attractin' attention to ourselves. We got our own work to do."

"We certainly have," the old man nodded emphatically. "Yuh didn't stop to see *El Liberador?*"

"Nope," Mort replied. "Figgered it wasn't necessary, and I wanted to let yuh know how we made out so we could hustle back south."

"Yuh did right," the old man said.

"Okay, suh, then we'll be ridin'."

They clumped out of the ranchhouse. Bridle irons jingled, saddle leather creaked and popped. Hoofs pattered on the hard surface of the trail. The old Captain went back to his fireplace and his dreams.

The silent troop rode away from the ranchhouse at a fast pace. They followed the gray trail that wound furtively between grove and thicket, past frowning cliff and swelling hill. For some miles they did not tighten rein. Then, at a word from the squat leader, they eased down to a smooth canter, slowed to a walk. Mort peered ahead into the shadows that fringed the edge of a bristle of growth and deepened to ebony solidity as the tall brush drew closer together. The troop slowed to a halt as a figure rode out of the shadows and held up a hand.

"That you, Boss?" Mort called, the intonation of his voice rather of statement than of question.

"Everything okay?" asked the newcomer in smoothly quiet tones.

"Uh-huh," Mort grunted.

"You saw Wallace?"

"Uh-huh, we stopped off at Captain Ben's place, per usual, and give him the lowdown. He was plumb pleased, per usual."

"Keep him that way," the other replied. "You got everything we need?"

"Everythin'," Mort replied. "Yuh shore everythin's lined up proper?"

"Am I in the habit of making mistakes?" the other retorted.

"Nope, vuh ain't," Mort conceded, "leastwise not yet. Hope yuh never do. One mite of a slip sometime and we're all liable to find ourselves dancin' on air."

"I don't make slips," the other replied shortly. "All right, let's get going. We haven't any time to waste. We must be in the clear before daylight."

Mort grunted something unintelligible. The other wheeled his horse. The group, thundering in his wake,

he vanished into the shadows. The beat of their horses'
irons dimmed away to the south.

*   *   *

The moon climbed the long slant of the sky, reached
the zenith and began its slow tumble toward the western horizon, and still Jim Hatfield slept, his head pillowed on his arms, his long body relaxed comfortably in
the big chair. The shadows beneath the trees deepened,
the silence of the night became more intense, until it was
broken by a faint whisper of footsteps on the grass, a
queer metallic scratching and a faint click, as of a door
bolt forced back under protest. The silence, closing down
like a sagging wall, was pregnant with expectancy.

Jim Hatfield awoke with a start, awoke to a feeling of
oppression, a heavy constriction about his chest, a stinging sensation in his nostrils. Drunken with sleep, he raised
his head from his numbed arms, his brain working slowly
and laboriously. Something, he sensed, was not as it
should be. Gradually, sound filtered through the fog of
sleep that still pressed down upon him. A dull crackling
that was oddly familiar. Almost mechanically he glanced
toward where his campfire must be burning with more
than usual intensity. It *must* be burning, he knew, for he
could smell the smoke. Only the bristle of tree branches
beyond the window sill met his bemused gaze. But the
whiff of burning wood persisted. Suddenly he shot wide
awake and reared erect in his chair. From somewhere beneath him had sounded a muffled explosion. Abruptly he
realized that while he was not stretched beside a campfire in the open, smoke was curling about his face. The
room was thick with it. He surged to his feet, gripped
frantically at the window ledge to keep from falling. His
legs had "gone to sleep" in his cramped position. They
were like two wooden posts and refused to support his
weight. He kept erect by clinging to the ledge and strove
to shake off the paralyzing cramp. He gritted his teeth

with the agony of renewing circulation as the "pins and needles" began to get in their work. He coughed and gagged from the smoke, thrust his head out the window, only to meet a cloud of it billowing up along the wall from below. On the ground outside was a reddish glow that swiftly grew in intensity.

He risked letting go of the ledge and staggered about drunkenly, making for the door. His legs were functioning something like normal by the time he reached it and cautiously opened it a crack. A wave of hot air gushed in, but he saw no flame. He opened the door wider, peered into the smoke filled hall. He stepped outside of the room and glanced along the hall toward the stairway that led to the living room. Tongues of flame were flickering up the well, and gushes of smoke.

"The whole downstairs must be on fire," he muttered as he slammed the door shut and leaped toward the open window. A glance out showed him that the ground was a long way off. To jump would be to guarantee death or serious injury. He turned to the bed, hauled off blankets and sheets. With swift, sure fingers he knotted them together, twisting and twining them. He shoved the heavy bedside against the wall and half blocking the window. A hitch around the stout bedpost and he had a line he felt sure would hold his weight dangling out the window. He swung a long leg across the sill, then abruptly halted.

"Old Caswell Klingman, the ranch owner," he exclaimed. "He aimed to sleep in the room at the head of the stairs! I wonder—"

He left the thought unfinished and swung his leg back into the room. He could recall no sound of moving about coming through the partition. Also, if Klingman had been aroused, he would surely have warned his guest before seeking to escape. Hatfield dashed across the room and flung the door wide.

Fire was roaring up the stairway, now, licking at

the corridor ceiling, running along the floor almost to the door of Klingman's room. Downstairs, above the roar of the flames, sounded a confused murmur of voices, and a pounding as of booted feet on the floor boards.

Hatfield raced along the hall to Klingman's door. The smoke was stifling. The heat made him gasp. He gripped the knob, turned it and flung the door open. The glow from the flames booming up the stairway reached into the room and showed a huddled form lying on the floor. It was old Klingman, half dressed, unconscious. Doubtless the ranch owner had been overcome by smoke before he was able to reach the door. Hatfield gathered the old man's bulky form into his arms, raised him without apparent effort and darted from the room. With the fire roaring along behind him, he reached his own room, slammed the door shut and leaped to the window. He uttered an exasperated oath.

Directly below the window was another that opened into the living room and not far from the foot of the stairs. From the lower window flame was gushing. It raced up the wall in a sheet. Only a charred length of some two or three feet remained of his hastily improvised rope. As he stared at it in dismay, he realized that figures were darting across the open space between the trees. One evidently spotted him at the window, by the glow of the flames. There was a flicker of steel, and as Hatfield instinctively leaped back, fire spurted through the shadows. There was the crash of a shot and the angry whine of a bullet that fanned his face with its lethal breath and spatted against the far wall.

"What in blazes!" yelped the bewildered Ranger as the figure vanished into the darkness. He was conscious of a wild yelling in back of the *casa*. Evidently the hands in the bunkhouse had been aroused.

But more pressing matters were at hand.

"Got to find another window," he muttered, and turned to the door.

A tongue of flame licked into the room the instant he opened it. He ducked his head and dashed through the fire. He sped along the hall to the nearest door, frantically turned the knob. It did not open.

"Locked," he muttered, and leaped to the next. The same result obtained, likewise with a third door on the opposite side of the hall. The last door, near the far end of the hall, also proved to be locked. He hurled his weight against the panels; they creaked and groaned; but the stout oaken planks sturdily resisted his efforts. He glanced wildly about, saw a stairway at the end of the hall, leading upward. He took the steps three at a time and found himself in the attic over the second floor, which ran the full length of the building. There was a window at either end, far up near the peak of the roof, and altogether out of reach. The eaves were low, however, and by standing close to the side wall he could reach the roof, the shingles of which were laid on stout longitudinal boards.

Placing Klingman's unconscious form on the floor, which was already hot to the touch, he drew his gun and jabbed at the shingles with the muzzle. They were dry and rotten and quickly crumbled under the assault. Soon he had a sizeable hole in the roof, through which poured welcome cool air. The aperture between the longitudinal boards, however, was too narrow to admit his body, and the boards were too strong to be battered away. The smoky air of the attic was stifling, the heat increasing by the second, blinding his eyes, sapping his strength. He glanced about for something that would serve as a battering ram, and found nothing. The attic was clear, save for several stout trunks scattered about.

Slanting the barrel of his gun, he fired shot after shot

into the lowest board. The heavy slugs slashed and splintered the wood. He jerked his second gun and continued to fire until a row of slanting bullet holes scored the board from side to side. Holstering the gun, he seized the weakened plank with both hands and swung his weight upon it. The board creaked and groaned, swayed inward. The weakened segment gave way, one severed end sagged downward. Hatfield put forth his strength and tugged desperately. The board bent to a bow, suddenly snapped, and left an opening several feet in length by perhaps thirty inches in width. Hatfield leaped to one of the trunks and dragged it beneath the opening. Then he picked up Klingman's body and climbed onto the trunk, thrusting his head and shoulders through the opening. He gulped in great draughts of the life giving air, and glanced about.

The roof had a steep pitch, but leveled off at the eaves where a stout copper gutter was bolted to the boards. Directly beneath was the spreading top of a great oak tree that drew near the house. The leaves obscured his view of the ground, from which came a chorus of shouts and curses. The glare of the flames glimmered upward through the branches. He could hear the roaring and crackling of the flames that were swiftly enveloping the entire house. To his dismay, and roof was considerably higher than the tree top, so that no projecting branch was within his reach.

"One chance, and a slim one, but I got to take it," he muttered, and ducked back into the stifling, smoke filled attic.

Exerting all his strength, he levered Klingman's limp body through the opening and let it rest on the slight offset above the gutter.

"Don't you come to now and roll off," he muttered as he climbed through the opening and crouched on the roof beside the unconscious rancher. For a tense moment he studied the tangle of branches immediately below.

Then he whipped off his stout neckerchief and securely bound Klingman's wrists together. He dragged the sagging form partially erect and managed to get the bound arms around his own neck. Bending over, teetering precariously on his narrow perch, he hunched Klingman onto his back. Then, taking a deep breath, he crouched still lower and leaped from the roof into the heart of the tangle of branches.

The slender upper limbs snapped under the double weight. They crashed through them and for a crawling instant Hatfield thought they were headed straight for the ground some thirty feet away. Then his clutching hand gripped a fairly stout limb. It bent under the strain, and snapped; but it broke the rush of the fall. He gripped another, which likewise broke. Then his chest came squarely across a third branch with a force that knocked the breath from his lungs. The branch creaked and bent, withstood the shock.

Waves of heat were boiling upward. The leaves were shrivelling in the torrid blasts; but the tree stood between windows and escaped the flames gushing from them.

For some moments Hatfield lay draped across the branch, crushed by Klingman's weight on his back, half strangled by the pressure of his bound wrists against his throat. Finally, however, he managed to get some air back into his tortured lungs and began to painfully inch along the branch toward the tree trunk. He reached it after what seemed an eternity of agonized effort and started clambering down the ladder rungs formed by the huge limbs. As he descended, the heat grew more intense. His body was drenched with sweat, his lungs were bursting. Hot flashes stormed before his eyes. He was trembling in every limb and his muscles seemed turning to water. Dimly he realized that men were running and shouting beneath the tree, that dark figures were climbing toward him. He felt hands gripping his body, lifting the intolerable burden from his back. Then all things were lost in a clammy blackness that enveloped him, wave on wave.

3

WHEN Jim Hatfield recovered consciousness, he was lying on the ground, some distance from the tree that had been his salvation. Nearby sat old Caswell Klingman, his head in his hands, and looking very sick indeed. Around them, their forms outlined in the glare of the blazing ranchhouse, were the Tumbling K cowboys, anxiously watching Clem Shore swab the Ranger's face with a damp cloth. They raised a whoop of joy as Hatfield opened his eyes.

"Gosh and blazes! feller," chattered Shore, "I figgered yuh were a goner! Take it easy, now, yuh had a close call."

Hatfield smiled faintly, and closed his eyes again as a wave of nausea swept over him. It passed quickly, however, and he took a chance on opening his eyes again. A moment later, with the assistance of Shore's arm, he struggled to a sitting position.

"Easy," cautioned the bewhiskered puncher. "How do yuh feel?"

"Sort of like I'd been dragged through a knothole and hung on a barbed wire fence to dry," Hatfield admitted.

"But I'll be okay in a minute," he added, flexing his stiff arms. He felt of his sore chest, winced at the pain caused by a deep breath; but from various symptoms he decided no bones were broken. A moment more and he got rather unsteadily to his feet and stood swaying.

25

Caswell Klingman also stood up. He stared at the Lone Wolf, stuck out his big hand.

"Much obliged," he said briefly. "I won't forget it."

"What happened?" Hatfield asked. "Something woke me up all of a sudden. Then there was a bang downstairs as if somebody had set off a handful of shotgun shells. I ran out to find the house on fire."

"The blankety-blank sidewinders blew the safe and set fire to the stairway, that's what," Clem Shore said grimly. "Reckon they figgered that by firin' the stairway just before they set off the charge, nobody could come down before they cleaned the safe. We hardly heard the explosion of the charge at the bunkhouse. By the time we'd figgered out what was goin' on they'd hightailed. Fact is, what set us scootin' out of our bunks was a gun shot we heard. Who was they shootin' at, do yuh know, Hatfield?"

In a few terse sentences, Hatfield explained the shot which had aroused the cowboys. He turned to Klingman.

"Much in the safe?" he asked.

"Better'n ten thousand dollars," the old rancher replied. "What I got for two big herds. I figgered on runnin' it to the bank tomorrow. The word sure got around fast· the buyer was here this afternoon."

"Any notion who's responsible?" Hatfield asked.

"The same bunch, I reckon, what's been raising hell hereabouts for quite a spell," Klingman returned. "Just who they are nobody seems to know. Come from down manana land, everybody figgers."

"By way of the Smugglers' Trail?" Hatfield asked, recalling the shadowy riders he had seen flitting through the mist of moonlight.

Klingman shrugged his shoulders.

"Could be," he admitted.

Hatfield nodded thoughtfully.

"Anybody got any notion what time it is?" he asked suddenly. "I've sort of lost count."

"Must be nigh onto three o'clock in the mornin'," Shore hazarded.

Hatfield nodded again, his eyes even more thoughtful. Evidently something like six hours elapsed between the time he saw the ghostly horsemen riding north and the attack on the ranchhouse.

Klingman gloomily eyed the burning building, which was now spouting flame from every direction.

"There goes a hell of a good *casa*," he growled. "Well, we'll start rebuildin' as soon as she cools off. Reckon the fust thing now is to break out that old stove in the storeroom and cook some breakfast. I could stand a cup of steamin' coffee. You hellions rustle me some clothes from the bunkhouse, and try and dig up a spare rainshed for Hatfield. Reckon he left his in the house. How come yuh took time to dress, son?"

Hatfield chuckled. "Was lucky enough to go to sleep in my chair before I undressed," he explained. "Glad I got a spare shirt in one of my saddlebags over to the barn. This one sort of took a beating."

"I'll ride to town come daylight and tell Sheriff White what happened—not that it will do any good," said Klingman. "Would like to have yuh ride with me, Hatfield, if yuh don't mind, seein' as you saw more of what went on than anybody else. Blazes! there goes the roof! She'll burn out before long, now. Yuh'll ride with me, son?"

Hatfield nodded agreement. The cowboys got busy dragging out the stove and preparing a meal from provisions cached in the storehouse. After a considerable helpin' and numerous cups of coffee, everybody felt somewhat better. The ranchhouse was now a smoldering heap of ruins. Amid the embers and still flickering beams and kingposts could be seen the massive iron safe, its door wrenched from the hinges. Robbery had undoubtedly been the motive back of the outrage.

As soon as it was light, Hatfield scouted the ground around the ranchhouse yard. He found where the raiders had left their horses to approach the building on foot.

"About a dozen, I'd say," he mused to himself. "That sort of tallies with the gents I saw riding north last night. What I'd like to know is where did they hole up for the six hours or so before they started operating here."

Shortly after sunrise, Hatfield and Klingman headed for town. All was quiet at the bee ranch when they reached the forks. Andy Cahil was nowhere in sight. The bees appeared to be going about their business in orthodox fashion.

Klingman chuckled reminiscently over the bee roping episode of the day before.

"Andy's a card," he said. "A cowhand who got a notion and cashed in on it. Money in bees, if yuh know how to handle 'em, and Andy seems to have a way with the critters. They won't sting *him*."

He coughed hoarsely and cleared his throat.

"Can't seem to get that blasted smoke out of my lungs," he complained. "There was a ventilator to my room from the lower floor, and I reckon the stuff sucked through it. The last thing I rec'lect is tumblin' out of bed in a room so thick yuh could cut out chunks with a knife. What I can't figger is how, big as yuh are, yuh managed to get me onto the roof and down that tree. I ain't no light weight. Son, yuh don't know yore own strength."

"It was mostly falling through the tree," Hatfield deprecated. "I just had to let go and tumble."

"Uh-huh, that's what I figger," Klingman returned dryly. "Only it was mighty ac'rate tumblin' without a busted neck at the end of it."

At the forks they turned north and rode across rolling rangeland. Hatfield gazed approvingly at the heavy stand of grass, the numerous groves and the not infrequent trickles of water.

"It's a reg'lar garden spot, this valley," Klingman observed. "Don't reckon there's any better range in the Big Bend country. Hills to right and left, and fencin' off the desert on the south. Plenty of cool canyons in the hills, and they provide shelter in bad weather. Was plumb peaceful hereabouts until late, too. Hell a-plenty been bustin' loose durin' the last couple of months. I've lost some cows, and the spreads north of here have lost more. Last night topped off everythin', though. I'd like to line sights with the sidewinders who did that. The sheriff and old Captain Ben Wallace will be fit to be tied when they hear about it. Old Ben sort of daddy's the section. Mebbe you've heard of him."

"The Ben Wallace who was brought up by General Sam Houston?" Hatfield asked, interested.

"That's right. He's always talkin' about General Sam. Figgers he was just about the greatest man what ever lived. Talks about him and his grand plan to form a separate country of Texas and New Mexico and Arizona and Mexico. He figgers Sam would have done it, if he hadn't died first."

"He would have tried," Hatfield agreed. "Mebbe General Sam was 'called' when he was just to prevent such a thing happening. It would have been mighty bad for Texas, suh."

Klingman nodded. "Chances are yuh're right," he agreed. "But back in those days lots of folks didn't think so. They had faith in General Sam and would have followed him through hellfire."

"A mistaken leader, even a just one, can do a powerful lot of damage," Hatfield returned gravely. "General Sam was mistaken, even though he did believe in his dream. There have been others before him, and there'll be others in the future. And always there is somebody ready to take advantage of the opportunity they present, often from purely selfish motives. Then everybody suffers."

Old Caswell Klingman bent a shrewd look on his young companion.

"Yuh're a funny feller, Hatfield," he said. "Sort of unusual for a wanderin' cowhand."

"Yes," Hatfield agreed smilingly, "for a wandering cowhand."

As they pursued their way into the north, other hills began to cut the horizon, misty with distance. Klingman observed Hatfield's gaze upon the towering crags.

"Those are the *Marajildas*," remarked Klingman, jerking his thumb toward the misty spires. "They're north of town about five miles. A little more and yuh can see the pass the trail takes to reach Como, the railroad town the other side of the hills. *Marajilda* Crik runs through the hills up there, curves south over west of here to reach the Big River. Runs through canyons and is a heller."

Hatfield nodded, eyeing the hills with interest.

"Smugglers' Trail run by way of there?" he asked.

"That's right," Klingman nodded. "She swings around Cibolero and joins with the track we're ridin' just this side of the hills. The old Hassayampa Trail to the west runs through 'em, only nobody rides it any more, since the railroad came along."

For some miles they rode in silence.

"Here's the end of my land," Klingman remarked at length. "Now we're on the Cross G. Ramon Garcia owns it."

The old rancher frowned darkly as he pronounced the name. Hatfield wondered why.

"North of the Cross G is Steve Tule's Four T," Klingman resumed. "Steve is a nice feller. Then comes Captain Ben Wallace's Barbed Five, biggest in the section. There are other smaller holdin's to the west and north of town, between here and the hills. The valley widens to the north. The Barbed Five runs for miles and miles to the east."

The sun was well up in the sky when they sighted the sprawling buildings of the town. As they drew near, Hatfield was conscious of a deep, rhythmic throbbing that quivered the air.

"Stamps," he observed.

"Right," replied Klingman. "The Monarch silver mine stamp mill is here in town; the mine is back in the hills to the west. She's a big one, the Monarch. Their weekly cleanup runs into thousands and thousands."

"Have they been losing any metal?" Hatfield asked.

Klingman chuckled. "Not the Monarch," he replied. "They're too smart for the owlhoots. They cast their silver bricks in hundred pound chunks. That's too much to pack on a horse's or a mule's back and get away with it. The jiggers would be run down before they could get in the clear. Nope, the Monarch ain't had any trouble with their output, though they did lose a payroll a while back. They run the bricks to Como in carts once a month. Send a couple of guards along for show, but they don't worry. Them's their buildin's up there on the shelf."

Hatfield eyed with interest the gaunt structures that housed the stamps and other machinery incidental to operating the mine. They dominated the town from their slightly elevated position. The trail ran in their shadow and became Cibolero's main street.

Some distance along the street they pulled up before the sheriff's office and entered. The peace officer was at his desk, glowering at a report. He nodded to Klingman, glanced suspiciously at Hatfield and cocked an attentive ear. He swore in wary disgust as Klingman outlined the happenings of the night before.

"The same bunch of sidewinders that took the Monarch payroll and wrecked the Sunset Flyer," he declared with conviction. "Nobody saw 'em, yuh say?"

"Hatfield here got a glimpse of 'em," Klingman replied, "but I don't reckon he saw 'em close enough to tell much."

The sheriff listened to what Hatfield had to say, and nodded gloomily.

"That damn Smugglers' Trail!" he growled. "They always travel by way of that!"

"Ever try keeping an eye on the trail?" Hatfield asked.

"I have," grunted the sheriff. "Twice I figgered I had the hellions cut off and ready for a loop, but each time they just nacherly didn't materialize where they were supposed to. Those hellions know every hole and crack in the section, even better than I do. I sometimes think it might be a local outfit instead of one from down below the Line, as everybody figgers. But I shore can't put my finger on any bunch hereabouts that could be pullin' the things they are."

"One man or two from the section could be directing operations," Hatfield remarked.

The sheriff nodded moodily. "I've thought of that," he admitted, "but still I can't figger anybody, that is, unless—"

He did not finish the sentence, but Hatfield saw him and Klingman exchange significant glances.

Sheriff White was a lanky oldtimer with sunken cheeks, a drooping mustache and frosty blue eyes. He looked capable, but the Lone Wolf sort of felt that he was behind the door when they handed out brains. A good type of Border peace officer who ran true to form, he decided. Put him in the middle of a shindig and he would be cool and efficient; but when it came to matching wits with such an outfit as was undoubtedly working the section, he was out of his element.

"I'll ride down to your place this afternoon and look around," the sheriff said. "Mebbe I can learn somethin', though I don't know what."

Klingman nodded gloomily. "I got to see about buildin' material," he said. "Got to throw some kind of a shack together. The boys are purty good with hammer and nails, so I reckon we'll make out somehow and build somethin' that'll keep the rain off. Damn them sidewinders, anyhow! I don't mind losin' the money so much, but burnin' my *casa* was somethin' else again. I'd give half my place just to line sights with them!"

Saying goodbye to the sheriff, Hatfield and Klingman left the office. As they stepped into the street, two ponderous carts, each drawn by four mules rumbled past. On either side of the carts rode an armed man.

"There goes the Monarch shipment to the railroad," said Klingman, gesturing toward the creaking carts. "Twenty bricks of a hundred pounds each in them two carts. And better'n a fifth of the metal is gold."

Hatfield whistled. "Something like a hundred and fifty thousand dollars represented," he remarked.

"That's right," replied Klingman. "The Monarch is about the biggest producin' mine in this section, mebbe in all Texas, I reckon. Them bricks are headed through the pass for the railroad."

"If somebody ever figgers a way to raid the shipment!" Hatfield mused.

"Nobody's packin' off a ton of metal on horseback," Klingman grunted. "And there ain't no other way to handle it fast enough so they'd have a chance at a get-away. The minute the carts pull out of town, the Monarch folks telegraph their agent at Como. They know mighty close just how long it takes for the carts to make the trip. If they don't show up right on schedule, armed men ride out of Como to find out why. Jiggers with their cayuses weighted down with them bricks would be overhauled in a hurry, pertickler as the only way out of the hills 'ceptin' by this trail or the Smuggler is over the Hassa-yampa Trail that runs through the hills, and it's a heller. They can't use the trail to Cibolero or the Smuggler 'cause all the way from the hills down here they run through open country and over spreads. They'd be spotted or headed off easy. Nope, the Monarch shipment is plumb foolproof."

Hatfield nodded thoughtfully. "Uh-huh," he commented, "too foolproof. I've experienced that 'foolproof' jobs are the easiest to upset when some smart jigger comes along and figgers the way to do it. Folks who are plumb sure they have all the holes plugged get careless."

"Could be," Klingman granted indulgently, "but I reckon this is the one where there ain't no holes. Let's drop in the Busted Flush here for a bite to eat. Breakfast this mornin' was sort of scrawny, and we et long before daylight. It lacks three hours of noon yet and we got plenty of time to 'tend to things. I want to have a talk with yuh, anyhow."

Hatfield offered no objection and they entered the Busted Flush, which proved to be a big saloon with a lunch counter, and tables for more leisurely diners. Klingman waved a cordial greeting to a very tall, very broad-shouldered and very handsome man who stood at the bar. His hair was black as Hatfield's own, his eyes also were black and his complexion was dark almost to swarthiness. His voice, when he returned Klingman's greeting was quiet and modulated.

"How's things over to the Four T, Steve?" Klingman asked.

"Fair to middling," the other replied. "And with you?"

"Oh, fine," Klingman grunted, "that is 'cept I was robbed of a hefty passel of dinero last night and my ranchhouse burned to the ground."

"What do you know!" exclaimed Steve. "How did it happen?"

In a few terse sentences, Klingman recounted the happenings of the night before. Steve shook his black head in wordless disapproval.

"Don't know what this country is coming to," he said.

Klingman growled his opinion of what it was "coming to," with a profane qualification as to the region.

"Steve," he added, "I want yuh to know Jim Hatfield, a young feller I've took a shine to. Jim, this is Steve Tule, who owns the Four T spread."

Tule acknowledged the introduction and shook hands with a firm grip. There was an inscrutable look in his black eyes as he raised them slightly to meet Hatfield's level gaze.

"See yuh later, Steve," Klingman said. "Jim and me are figgerin' a little surroundin'. Care to join us?"

"I ate early," Tule replied.

"Steve's a plumb nice feller," Klingman said as he led the way to a table. "Everybody's learned to like him since he showed up here a coupla years back. He has an interest in this place, and owns some stock in the Monarch. His ranch is one of the best run spreads in the section."

"Texan?" Hatfield asked. Klingman shook his head.

"Nope. From back East—Kentucky I understand he said."

Hatfield nodded, and looked thoughtful, but did not comment. He continued to regard the tall Tule for some moments.

"I've seen that jigger somewhere before," he told himself. "Seen him, or somebody that sure looks a heap like him. Funny, the way it comes to me. Seem to see him standing sort of like he is now, looking off into the distance. Can't recall anything else about him, but sure can't help feeling that I *have* seen him before."

With a shrug of his shoulders he dismissed the matter, which doubtless was of no significance, after all.

They gave their orders to a waiter and lounged comfortably in their chairs to smoke until the food arrived. Klingman eyed his companion speculatively.

"Hatfield," he said at length, "I meant what I said when I told Steve Tule I'd taken a shine to you. I have, and I want to say something to yuh. I can use another tophand about yore build. I pay good wages—a mite above the average, and workin' conditions ain't bad. Of course you and me would have to bunk in the barn until we get another *casa* throwed together, but I've a notion yuh've slept in rougher quarters at times. What yuh say?"

"Well," smiled the Ranger, "I've known worse beds than blankets on good clean hay, and it won't take over long to get a new ranchhouse put up. Reckon I could do worse."

"Fine!" applauded Klingman at the oblique acceptance of the proffered job. "Let's have a drink on it." He signalled the waiter.

As they discussed the whiskey, the swinging doors swayed open and a man entered, glancing keenly about. Caswell Klingman frowned blackly.

"And there," he said in low tones, jerking his thumb toward the newcomer, "is in my opinion what's at the bottom of all the hell raisin' hereabouts."

Hatfield eyed the new arrival with interest. He was a rugged finely set up man with regular features, blue eyes and crisply curling golden hair. There were certain details of his dress that set him apart from the sprinkling of cowhands and others, in the place. His bearing was assured, almost arrogant, as he strode lithely to the bar; but his smile was pleasant enough when he greeted the bartender and his speech was soft and courteous.

"Who is he?" Hatfield asked.

"*Don* Ramon Garcia, or so he calls himself," growled Klingman. "An oiler, of course. He owns the Cross G."

Hatfield thoughtfully surveyed Garcia, his black brows drawing together slightly.

"Spanish, I'd say," he remarked. "Blue-eyed, blonde Spaniard, from northern Spain, or Navarre, the chances are."

"They're all oilers to me," grunted Klingman, casting a glance of distaste toward Garcia's broad back.

"Nothing wrong with Mexicans," Hatfield replied quietly. "Some mighty fine folks come from below the Line; but that gent is just as liable as not to be a descendant of the kings or princes of Castilian Spain or the old kingdom of Navarre."

"Still an oiler," growled Klingman, stubbornly, "and I don't like him. He's too darn uppity. Him and Steve Tule don't get along."

Hatfield nodded, apparently not particularly surprised at the information. He had already noted the clash of glances between the two big men.

"A rapier blade and a cavalry sabre," he mused to himself apropos of the steely looking Tule and the massive Garcia. "I've a notion sparks aplenty fly when they cross."

After the single hostile glance, however, Tule and Garcia ignored one another. The waiter placed filled dishes on the table and Klingman and Hatfield set to with the application of men who have known what it is to find good food scarce.

4

MEANWHILE the silver carts rolled steadily northward. Ahead the frowning ramparts of the Marajilda
Hills loomed clearer and clearer against the sky, with the
dark notch of the pass cleaving the cliffs and the swelling
slopes like a mighty sword cut.

The carts proceeded at a steady pace, the two guards
ambling alongside, their reins loose, their horses taking
it easy. It was a carefree procession; the guards, with
nothing to worry about, laughed and chaffed with the
drivers and one another. The trail wound smoothly on, a
gray ribbon in a setting of green.

Nearer and nearer drew the hills, until from the east
another ribbon of trail edged toward the Cibolero. It was
the old Smuggler Trail. While from the west, flowing
snakily from a canyon mouth, came the even older Hassayampa Trail, the freighting route to the west before the
railroad north of the hills made it unnecessary.

The carts drew near the spot where the three trails
joined to continue as one through the pass and so on to
Como, the railroad town. Here the chaparral grew high
and thick, a dark bristle of tangled branches.

The carts reached the junction. The drivers settled
themselves on their seats for the long pull up the slope
to the notch. The guards slowed their horses in anticipation of the toil of the incline. The bristle of growth stood
stiff and silent.

And then from the recesses of that silent growth burst a storm of gunfire. One guard slumped from his saddle and lay without sound or motion. The other, reeling in his hull, blood spouting from his left shoulder, gamely went for his gun. A second roaring volley and he pitched to the ground beside his companion. One driver fell backward upon the bricks stacked in his cart, his breast rent and shattered by slugs. The second driver rose to his feet, whirled about and fell over the side of the cart. Prone in the dust he lay, blood pouring from a blue hole in his forehead just at the hairline and visoring his face with scarlet.

Out of the brush dashed ten masked horsemen. Some caught the plunging mules and quieted them, while others approached the fallen guards and drivers, guns out and ready.

"All done for," one announced.

"Good!" growled a squat, brawny individual who appeared to be the leader of the band. "All right, now, get busy and transfer them bricks. Sift sand, too, for we haven't any time to waste."

The owlhoots swung to the ground and began hauling the ponderous ingots from the carts. Behind each man's saddle, a crude aparejo or pack saddle sagged down across his horse's flanks. Into either pocket of the packs an ingot was thrust. The horses protested violently against the overloading, but were subdued.

Busy at their task, none noticed the lashes of the bloody-faced driver flutter, nor the sideways glint of eyes between his slitted lids.

The carts emptied, the masked band mounted, mastering their plunging horses with difficulty. They turned into the Hassayampa Trail and rode off at a slow pace, the burdened cayuses still protesting the heavy loads banging against their flanks.

When the thud of hoofs on the trail had ceased to be

audible, the driver raised his bloody head, groaned, and floundered to his hands and knees. After a moment of struggle he got to his feet, reeling and swaying drunkenly. He raised a trembling hand to his wound.

"Just creased," he muttered thankfully. "Slug skidded along the bone and come out the top of my head. If I don't bleed to death, I'll make it."

Stumbling and floundering, he reeled to where the horses of the slain guards stood patiently by the side of the trail. After several futile attempts, he managed to mount one. Sagging forward onto the animal's neck, he twined his fingers in the coarse mane and started down the trail. Bleeding, moaning with pain, little more than half conscious, he rode toward Cibolero.

After finishing their meal, Hatfield and Klingman went about the business of contracting for lumber and other building materials. This chore completed, they headed back to the sheriff's office.

"We'll ride down to the spread with White," Klingman said. "Not that there's much sense of him going down there, but I reckon he feels he'd ought to."

They were nearing the office when a clatter of hoofs sounded ahead. Down the main street rode a bloody-faced man wild of eye, mouthing incoherently. He jerked his mount to a sliding halt before the sheriff's office. Hatfield sprang forward and caught him as he slumped limply from the saddle. Cradling the moaning driver in his long arms, he carried him into the office and laid him on a bunk.

"Water," he directed the yammering sheriff, "and some whiskey, if you've got it."

He took the bottle the sheriff proffered, raised the muttering man and set the neck against his lips.

"Take a pull of this, feller," he said.

The driver managed to swallow a mouthful. He

coughed, sputtered, quieted somewhat. In a few moments the liquor began to have its effect and he was babbling forth his story of the robbery.

The sheriff swore exultantly. "We've got 'em!" he cried. "They can't make any speed with those heavy loads, and they ain't got much more than an hour's start. They must have figgered Hank here was done for and that they had plenty of time to get in the clear. I know a short-cut to the Hassayampa. I'll get a posse together in twenty minutes and we'll be right on their tails. Hatfield, you look after Hank. Klingman, hustle down to Doc McChesney's office and bring him here while I round up the boys. I'd like to have yuh both ride with me."

In somewhat less than the twenty minutes, the old frontier doctor was cleansing and bandaging the driver's wound and the sheriff had his men ready to ride. With loose rein and busy spur, the posse thundered out of Cibolero.

The sheriff led the way across the rangeland to where the hills curved south. Over a faint track they climbed the slopes, bored through a defile and descended the far sag. Within less than an hour they struck the Hassayampa Trail.

"I figgered so," exulted the sheriff, pointing to deeply scarred hoof marks in the soft surface of the trail. "It rained hard yesterday morning and the sun don't get to this track much. Trailin' the sidewinders will be easy as fallin' off a slick log."

"They're not making any speed," Hatfield agreed, studying the hoof prints.

At a swift pace the posse rode southward along the trail. Soon, however, it began to veer to the west. A little later and they were riding the bank of a dark, fairly wide stream that flowed southward.

"Marajilda Crik," the sheriff said to Hatfield. "The trail crosses it about a mile farther on. There's a ford, the only

place yuh can cross for thirty miles. The trail runs on
west. The crik dives into a canyon and runs south
through the hills. Uh-huh, it's nigh onto thirty miles before it came out of that hole. Then it runs for a couple
of miles across a flat and dives into another canyon.
Don't come out again till the hills peter out over to the
southwest, at the edge of the desert. The Marajilda runs
into the Rio Grande over close to the north mouth of
Saint Helena Canyon."

With the deeply scored hoof marks assuring them they
were on the right track, the posse rode swiftly, their eyes
to the front. Jim Hatfield alone appeared to take greater
interest in his immediate surroundings, the clumps of
growth, the frowning cliffs and the grim chimney rocks.
Always, however, his glance came back to the hoof
prints in the trail, which he continued to study intently.

Abruptly the trail swerved, turning from southwest
to almost due west, heading straight for the edge of the
dark water. Here the east bank was low, and a few dozen
yards south of the trail, was soft and muddy. The trail,
following a harder strata, ran to the water's edge. On the
far bank it continued, climbing the shelving slope, which
was composed of naked rock.

Into the water splashed the posse, riding in single file.

"Careful," cautioned the sheriff, "the ford is narrow and
there's deep water on either side. Slip off and yuh'll hafta
swim for it."

The crossing was made without mishap, however, the
water never rising above the cinch straps. They clattered
up the far bank, across a stony stretch of perhaps a fifth
of a mile and onto the soft earth of the trail once more.
But before they had ridden another hundred yards, Jim
Hatfield's voice rang out, abruptly, preemptory.

"Hold it!" he shouted. "Hold it! We've been outsmarted!"

The posse jostled to a halt, volleying questions.

"What's the matter with yuh, son?" demanded the sheriff. "Them hellions came this way—there's the hoof prints leadin' on in front."

"Yes," Hatfield replied quietly, "*they* came this way; but the silver bricks stopped off somewhere?"

"What in blazes do yuh mean?" yelped the sheriff. "How yuh know?"

"Look at the hoof prints," Hatfield replied. "They're not near as deep as they were the other side of the crik, and look at the distance between the marks. See how the horses have lengthened their strides. That bunch is travelling twice as fast as they were the other side of the crik. They're going at top speed, which they'd never be able to with those silver bricks bogging them down."

The sheriff swore luridly.

"Hell and blazes! Yuh're right!" he declared. "But what became of the bricks? They packed 'em right to the water's edge, that's sure for certain. Did they chuck 'em into the crik?"

"Mebbe," Hatfield replied, "but I don't think so."

He glanced ahead, studying the trail.

"To run down that bunch ahead will be a chore," he said. "They've got a good start, and the chances are they know every crack and hole in these hills. "I've a notion they'd give us the slip, especially if they manage to keep ahead of us till dark, which they're mighty liable to do. I suggest we try and find out what became of the metal."

The sheriff swore some more. "Okay," he growled agreement. "If yuh've got a notion, let's hear it. I'm stumped, and I admit it."

"Back across the crik," Hatfield directed. "We'll see what we can find out."

They forded the stream once more and paused at the far edge of the water. Hatfield dismounted, glanced keenly about, and started walking down stream, studying the ground. He crossed the rocky strip that accommodated the ford and onto the muddy flat beyond. Abruptly he paused.

"I thought so," he exclaimed exultantly to the posse members, who were stringing along behind him. He pointed to a deep, wedge-shaped indentation in the soft earth at the water's edge.

"Made by the prow of a boat," he explained. "They had a boat tied up here waiting. They stopped off and loaded the silver into it. Look at all the boot tracks here by the water's edge. Yes, they loaded the metal into a boat and sent it down stream. Then they crossed the crik and rode on along the Hassayampa to make a false trail for a posse to follow. They know just exactly what they're about."

The sheriff's face turned purple and he appeared to breathe with difficulty. Hatfield paid no attention to these alarming symptoms. His glance was following the course of the stream, which, less than a mile farther on, vanished into the dark mouth of a canyon.

"The current isn't very swift," he mused, almost to himself.

"Yuh mean to ride downstream after the blankety-blank-blanks?" bawled the sheriff. "That water's ten feet deep and there ain't no bank inside that blankety-blank canyon."

"No," Hatfield replied, "but there's a chance we might get ahead of the slow moving boat and be ready for them when they come out of the canyon at the flat down to the south you told me about. You know how to get south through the hills without taking too much time?"

"By gosh, I do!" exclaimed the sheriff. "Back along the trail a half mile is a way through the hills to the Cibolero Trail. Then about five miles south of Andy Cahil's bee ranch is a fork that'll take us to the flats where the crik comes out of the canyon. If we can make the flats before the boat does, we'd ought to be all set. Let's go!"

At top speed the posse headed back up the trail. They

turned into a narrow defile that wound through the hills and eventually reached the broad surface of the Cibolero Trail, along which they sped south. Mile after mile they covered in grim silence, while the sun slanted westward and the shadows grew long. They flashed past Cahil's bee ranch and raced onward. Their horses flecked with foam and blowing hard, they reached the fork of which White had spoken, turned into it and approached the dark loom of the hills. Close to their base ran the narrow thread that appeared to be little more than a game track. Ahead loomed a towering promontory that Sheriff White said flanked the flat on the south. They rounded a beetling bulge of cliff and the flat, really the mouth of a very wide canyon, was before them. Gushing from its gorge they saw Marajilda Creek.

They saw more. Perhaps half a mile distant, bobbing along in the middle of the stream, was a flat-bottomed boat of considerable size containing three men, one of whom bent his weight to a long sweep with which he steered the unwieldy craft.

The possemen let out an exultant whoop and urged their flying horses to greater speed. Swiftly they bore down upon the slower moving craft, which was headed for the dark canyon mouth a mile or more distant. As they drew within easy rifle range, the sheriff let out a stentorian bellow.

"Steer that thing to the shore if yuh don't want to eat lead!" he boomed.

The three men, who had been glancing over their shoulders at the approaching horsemen, crouched low. Puffs of smoke gushed from the boat, slugs whined past the possemen.

"Let 'em have it—they ain't goin' to stop!" the sheriff ordered grimly.

Instantly the possemen let loose with their rifles. One of the boatmen flung erect, wavered, pitched over the side into the dark waters of the stream. The other two continued to fire. The boat drew ever nearer the dark mouth of the canyon.

Again the possemen used their rifles. One cursed as an answering bullet creased his arm. Then they lowered their smoking weapons and stared at the crumpled figures lying silent and motionless across the stacked silver bricks. The boat, its unmanned steering sweep swinging wildly, swept onward toward the canyon mouth.

"The blankety-blank-blanks!" roared the sheriff. "They done outsmarted us after all. There's rapids in that canyon and she'll never ride 'em. With nobody steerin' she'll bust up on the rocks shore as blazes. The silver is a goner!"

The cursing possemen pulled their horses to a halt. All but Jim Hatfield. His voice rang out like a golden bugle—

"Trail, Goldy! Trail!"

Instantly the great sorrel extended himself. Like a flickering sunbeam he flashed across the flat, heading toward where within a few yards of the canyon's mouth, a long fang of rock extended almost to midstream. Before the possemen divined Hatfield's intention, Goldy's irons were clashing on the flat surface of the ledge. Where it narrowed, Hatfield pulled him to a halt, leaped from the saddle and ran nimbly to the very point of the spit, where he poised, leaning forward, his eyes fixed on the approaching boat.

"He's goin' to try and jump into her!" whooped the sheriff. He let out another whoop as Hatfield bent his legs and launched his long body through the air. The possemen bellowed a cheer as he landed on the pile of silver bricks, reeled, caught his balance by a miracle of agility and turned toward them.

"I'll beach her where the crik comes out the canyon," he shouted. "Try and follow me by the trail."

"We'll foller, but it's a long way around," the sheriff

yelled back. "Good luck, son. Hope the rapids don't get yuh!"

He waved his hand in goodbye as the lurching craft vanished into the gloom of the canyon mouth.

5

HATFIELD clambered across the bricks to the stern of the boat, stepping over the bodies of the slain owl-hoots, and seized the handle of the steering sweep, which fortunately was secured in place by an oarlock. Steadying the boat, he glanced about.

The sun was low in the sky and it was already quite dark in the depths of the canyon; but he could see that the waters of the stream washed the smooth rock walls on either side, with no intervening strip of beach. He noted, too, that the speed of the current was perceptibly increasing. Soon he became conscious of a low murmuring that swelled to a mutter, a rumble, a deep-toned roar that vibrated between the walls.

"Rapids," he muttered. "Big ones, too, with plenty of rocks, and I don't know the channel. This is going to be touch-and-go!"

He peered ahead, narrowing his eyes, bending his weight against the handle of the sweep. Soon he could see the white froth where the water spouted foam from the black rocks that fanged above its surface. His lean jaw tightened, the muscles of arm and back stood out under his shirt as he gripped the steering oar.

Like living monsters full of menace, the black fangs of stone rushed toward him. The boat tossed and rocked as it struck the beginning of the rapids. All about was swirling black water, gusts of spray, jagged horns of rock.

Frenziedly working the sweep, Hatfield strove to steer the unwieldy craft between the deadly ledges. Once a projecting horn of rock planed off a long, curling shaving the entire length of the planks. Again, he felt the grind of submerged stone rasping the boards beneath him. They struck a rounded cone a glancing blow that made the planks creak. A half submerged flat rock reared the bow high in the air and for a terrible moment, Hatfield was sure that boat would capsize. But it slid off the obstacle and continued its wild progress down the stream. He heaved a vast sigh of relief as they shot through the final fringe of the rapids and surged into quiet water once more.

For several miles the stream ran swiftly and smoothly between its rock walls. Then again the ominous mutter foretold another and even longer rapid. Soon Hatfield saw the ghostly fringe of spray that spouted from the rocks jutting above the surface. And then the scene of danger and difficulty was repeated, more hazardous than before, because of the thickening gloom. More than once, Hatfield was certain that his death by drowning was at hand. Finally, however, he cleared the rough water and careened downstream. It was with devout thankfulness that he at last noted that the side walls were lowering in indication of nearing the canyon's end. A little later he boomed out of the gorge mouth and saw the rolling rangeland opening out before him.

The west bank of the stream was still precipitous, but that on the east was low and thickly grown with tall chaparral. Using the sweep as an oar, he maneuvered the craft to the shore and beached her on a little sandy strip between the growth and the water's edge. He stepped out; stretching his cramped limbs and glancing about. He stiffened as a harsh voice spoke from the growth.

"All right, feller, get yore hands up. Yuh're covered!"

Glancing swiftly in the direction of the voice, Hatfield saw the ominous glint of a rifle barrel trained at his breast. He slowly raised his hands shoulder high.

From the dark bristle of growth stepped four men, eyes alert, guns ready. They paused, and stared at the Ranger.

"Hell and blazes!" one exclaimed. "If it ain't the feller the Boss was tellin' us about, I'm an oiler. Say, you, how in tarnation did yuh come to be in that boat?"

"Never mind that," another broke in in tones of authority. "He wouldn't tell yuh, and we ain't got no time for foolin'. Tie him up. The Boss will find out from him, when he sees him; I've a notion he'll be almighty glad to see him. And this hellion will be glad to answer questions before the Boss gets through with him, too. Turn around, you, and keep yore hands where they are. Tie him up, Cliff, and set him over there with his back against that rock. We got to get that stuff out the boat and loaded before somebody comes snoopin' around here. I don't like the looks of things. Get goin'!"

A moment later Hatfield heard one of the men approach behind him. His gun belt was removed. In obedience to a harsh order, he lowered his hands. They were securely tied behind him. Then he was shoved toward the rock in question and ordered to squat. A cord was passed around his ankes and drawn tight.

"Hustle," ordered the man who appeared to be the leader. "It's almost dark."

One of the men entered the brush. The other three approached the boat. They swore venomously and cast black looks at Hatfield as they viewed the two bodies slumped across the silver bricks. They rifled the pockets of the dead men, removed their guns and callously dumped the bodies into the stream. Meanwhile a string of pack mules had been led from the brush. The silver bricks were removed from the boat and loaded onto

the mules. Then horses were led out, including three
spares, evidently intended for the individuals who had
manned the boat. Hatfield's ankles were loosed, he was
ordered to mount. His legs were securely bound to the
stirrup straps.

The cavalcade got under way in the last light of the
dying day. They wound south, then turned west and
skirted the lower slopes of the hills for many miles, finally
turning into a narrow gorge. In almost total darkness
they proceeded for several more miles, pausing at last
before a stoutly built cabin almost hidden by growth.
Here the owlhoots dismounted. A lamp was lighted in
the cabin. The mules were unloaded and the bricks carried inside. Finally mules and horses were hobbled and
allowed to graze. Hatfield was untied from his horse and
ordered into the cabin. He found himself in a fairly commodious room outfitted with bunks along the wall, a
rusty cook stove, a table and several chairs. There were
some cooking utensils on shelves and some coarse crock-
ery. Also a supply of staple provisions. Evidently the
cabin was frequently used.

"Cliff, yuh'll stay here and keep a eye on this hellion,"
the leader ordered. "The rest of us will be ridin' to join
the Boss. He'll want to know about this pronto. We'll be
back tomorrow night, with the Boss, after dark. We'll un-
tie this hellion and shove him into the other room. Be
sure yuh keep the door locked. Don't take no chances
with him. Never mind if he gets a mite hungry. He won't
have long to be hungry once the Boss gets here. Keep him
locked up. He's plumb pizen, if he's the jigger we figger
him to be. Okay, you, turn around till I can cut yuh loose.
Then through that door over there."

Hatfield obeyed. His bonds were cut and he was
shoved through the door in question. It banged shut
after him. He heard the click of a shot bolt. There was a

rumbling of voices in the outer room, then the bang of the closing outer door. It was followed by a click of horses' irons, fading swiftly into the distance.

Hatfield proceeded to take stock of his surroundings. There was a crack perhaps a half-inch wide between the door and the jamb where it was hinged to the wall, and through this crack light streamed from the outer room. Its dim glow revealed that he was in a room much smaller than the one he had just quit It boasted a single window stoutly barred with iron, a bunk built against the far wall, but no other article of furniture. He crossed to the bunk, smoothed out the tumbled blankets and sat down. His matches and tobacco had been left him, so he fished out the makin's and rolled a cigarette. For some time he smoked thoughtfully, going over the situation in his mind.

That he was in a very tight spot was painfully evident. The mysterious "Boss" apparently knew him, was perhaps acquainted with his Ranger connections. At any rate, the boss considered him decidedly a menace, and as such, doubtless, a fit subject for extermination. Hatfield had already developed a disquieting theory relative to himself from the apparently senseless firing of the Tumbling K ranchhouse and the bullet sent with deadly aim through the window. Now, it would seem, he was in the power of the sinister band that stopped at nothing to achieve their ends. The ruthless killing of the guards and the driver of the silver carts was evidence enough of their utter callousness. He could expect no mercy at their hands. His only chance was to escape before the Boss arrived on the scene the following night. And from present appearances, that was impossible.

Pinching out the butt of his cigarette, he arose and crossed softly to the window. The bars that criss-crossed the opened window were firmly imbedded in the heavy beams that framed the window. They were of half-inch iron, and not even his strength could hope to move them. The walls were of stout logs fitted closely together. The floor planks were thick slabs of oak. The door was also of stout planks and securely bolted on the outside. Stout strap hinges secured it to the jamb; the heavy screws holding the hinges in place were deeply driven into the wood. There was nothing in the room that would serve as a battering ram with which to break his way out, even if the armed guard should absent himself, which doubtless he had no intention of doing. Hatfield went back to the bunk and sat down once more.

In the outer room he could hear his guard moving about, apparently building a fire and preparing to cook a meal. Soon the tantalizing aroma of boiling coffee and frying bacon drifted into the hungry Ranger. Hatfield grinned philosophically, and rolled another cigarette. He continued to smoke, and think, while the guard ate his supper and washed the dishes. He made a trip or two outside, doubtless for water, but each time was gone but a few minutes. While he was out, Hatfield slipped to the door and peered through the crack. He could see his own guns and belts hanging from a peg. His knife and other possessions that had been taken from him lay on the table. He gazed longingly at the long-barrelled Colts. They seemed almost within arm's reach, but they might have been on the other side of Texas, for all the chance he had of laying hands on them. He slid back to the bunk as the guard entered the room, closing the door behind him.

For some time Hatfield heard him moving about. Then came the thump of his boots on the floor as he removed them. The light dimmed as he turned the lamp low. A bunk creaked under his weight. Hatfield heard him yawn noisily a few times; then gradually there was silence, which was presently broken by a steady, rhythmic rumble. The guard was fast asleep and snoring.

Hatfield got to his feet again and crossed to the window. He peered through the bars; but by the faint starlight of the still moonless night, he could see little other than the dark mass of the chaparral growing close to the cabin wall.

The night was deathly still, the silence broken only by an occasional stamp or snort on the part of one of the mules or horses hobbled nearby. From back in the black depths of the canyon came the lonely, beautiful plaint of a hunting wolf. An owl perched in the top of some blasted pine answered the call with a querulous whine. A small wind mourned softly in the branches. The leaves rustled, making a mournful music. Then the silence closed down, save for the steady snoring of the owlhoot in the outer room.

Hatfield gazed out the window a moment longer. The sky to the east was brightening. Soon there would be a moon. He turned and crossed to the door and examined it with meticulous care. The bolt that held it shut was undoubtedly a ponderous affair. The boards were stout and thick. He ran his fingers aimlessly over them. His nails rasped on the rough surface of the iron strap hinge. Absently, he inserted a nail into the slot in the head of one of the screws, running it back and forth in the groove.

Suddenly he stiffened, his eyes widening. The screw felt a trifle loose. Swiftly he examined the others that held the hinge in place. They appeared tight enough; but that one loose fastening indicated that the wood of the jamb might be slightly rotten. If so, it might be possible to move the screws. That is if he had something to serve as a screwdriver. His knife, which might have served, had, of course been taken from him. It lay on the table in the outer room. He crossed to the bunk and pulled off the blankets, hoping that there might be a sharp strap or plate that would answer his purpose. The bunk was put together with nails and wooden pins. The room was utterly empty of other furnishings. He straightened up, staring at the door, his mind working furiously. Suddenly he uttered a low exclamation. His hands flew to his broad leather belt, fumbled for a moment with a cunningly concealed secret pocket. He drew forth something that glittered in the beam of light—a silver star set on a silver circle! The badge of the Texas Rangers.

Hatfield turned the badge over in his slim fingers. It was stoutly made. The heavy silver plating, he knew, was backed by steel. The rounded edge was just thin enough to fit into the slot in the head of the screw. He tried it on the loose one. A few moments of turning and the screw came out of the wood. He set it aside and tackled another.

The second screw proved to be a different matter. It resisted his efforts stubbornly. Finally, however, after what seemed an eternity of effort, it moved a little. Another turn and it loosened perceptibly. Soon he had it free from the wood.

But there were four screws in each of the straps that secured the hinges to the jamb. Before the last screw was out, Hatfield was drenched with sweat and trembling in every limb. His fingers were sore and bleeding. The rim of the badge bent out of shape all around its perimeter. When the final stubborn cylindrical shank came free, and the door sagged slightly against the jamb, Hatfield, after making sure the door would remain in place, staggered to the bunk and sank upon it, utterly exhausted.

For a long time he sat motionless on the bunk, till his strength returned. Then he cautiously approached the door again. The guard continued to snore in the outer room. No other sound disturbed the silence. He carefully inserted his fingers into the crack between the door and the jamb and tugged gently. The door creaked, swayed inward. With the greatest care he drew it toward him a little more, until he could get a firm grip on the boards. Then, summoning his strength, he wrenched mightily. The bolt came free with a metallic screech. Hatfield jerked the door inward and hurled it to the floor. It hit the boards with a thunderous crash. Hatfield bounded through the opening and toward the bunk. The guard, shot from his slumbers, let out a wild yell. Hatfield caught a gleam of metal and swerved sideways. The guard's gun blazed in his face. He felt the wind of the passing bullet. He hurled himself upon the man, and before the guard, still half dazed with sleep, could pull the trigger a second time, fingers like rods of nickel steel gripped his wrist, grinding the bones together. He yelled a second time, with the intolerable pain, and lashed out wildly with his free hand, catching Hatfield a terrific blow on the jaw. For a moment red flashes stormed before the Ranger's eyes and blackness threatened to engulf him. The gun, its muzzle pointing upward, exploded again, the bullet thudding into the ceiling boards. Hatfield shot out his free hand and gripped the weapon by the lock. The guard battered at him with his fist, butted with his head, kicked and thrashed. He rolled out of the bunk onto his feet. Hatfield wrenched at the gun. He stepped on a greasy spot on the floor, his boot slipped and he fell. He hit the floor with a crash, but managed to hold onto the gun, which was wrenched from the guard's hand. As the owlhoot leaped at him, bellowing with maniacal fury, Hatfield shot from the hip.

The guard halted as if struck by a mighty fist. He reeled back, staggered, pitched forward onto his face. He writhed for a moment, making queer bubbling sounds in his throat, stiffened, relaxed, and lay still.

Watchfully alert, Jim Hatfield staggered to his feet, breathing in great gasps, his head spinning. By an iron effort of the will he kept his eyes focused on the body of the guard, holding the gun ready for instant use.

But the owlhoot did not move. He lay perfectly quiet, not even a finger twitching. Hatfield stepped forward and bent over him. Then he straightened up with a mutter of relief. The guard was dead.

Hatfield's first act was to retrieve and buckle on his gun belts. He carefully examined his guns, making sure they were loaded and in perfect working order. He pocketed his other possessions, which lay on the table, evidently awaiting the arrival of the Boss for ultimate disposal.

Coals still glowed in the stove. He raked them together and put in fresh fuel. There was a half pot of coffee, plenty of bacon ready to hand and a plate of biscuits left over from the dead guard's supper. Hatfield warmed up the coffee and prepared a meal, which he sorely needed. Then he smoked a cigarette and took stock of the situation.

To remain in the cabin was impractical. Doubtless the Boss would bring the rest of the band with him and the odds would be too great for even the Lone Wolf to cope with. He had not the vaguest notion where he was, but gathered from Sheriff White's last shouted remark, and the distance travelled from where he beached the boat, that he was a very long ways from town. And it was already well past midnight. He grimly eyed the stacked silver bars, and arrived at a decision.

"The hellions won't get that, anyhow," he told himself.

Before setting to work on the silver bricks, Hatfield carefully examined the body of the dead guard. He was a hard looking character with little to set him apart other than a viciousness of expression and a peculiar blotched condition of his skin. The Ranger turned out his pockets systematically, and discovered little of interest. A plump tobacco pouch showed up, among other things.

"Reckon I can use this," Hatfield muttered. "My stock is getting sort of low."

He opened the pouch and sniffed at the contents. Suddenly his eyes narrowed. He sniffed again, wrinkling his nostrils as in distaste. He took a pinch of tobacco from the pouch and dropped it on the glowing coals in the stove. Smoke arose, smoke that gave off a peculiar odor, something like scorched cheese.

"Well, I'll be darned," the Ranger muttered. He stared at the pouch, closed it and tucked it into his pocket. He glanced around the cabin with quickened interest. A bulky cupboard, built of rough boards, that stood near the stove, caught his eye. He crossed to it and opened the closed door.

The contents of the cupboard were surprising. The lamp light gleamed on the parallel barrels of more than two dozen rifles standing in orderly rows. A quick examination assured Hatfield that they were all brand new and all of the very latest pattern. None, he ascertained had been fired since leaving the manufacturer's testing range. Stacked beside the rifles were half a dozen cases of ammunition.

"Somebody sure is going in for good guns, and plenty of 'em," he mused as he closed the cupboard door. "Wonder what else I can find?"

However, a careful survey of the cabin revealed nothing else of interest. Hatfield gave over the search and set to work on the silver.

The hobbled mules afforded no difficulty; but loading the twenty hundred pound ingots into their pack saddles was an exhausting task. Finally, however, it was done. Hatfield caught one of the horses, got saddle and bridle on it and mounted. Leading the string of laden mules, he set out down the canyon. Dawn was brightening the sky before he reached its mouth. Here he turned east, skirting the base of the hills toward where, how far off he could not tell, he knew the Cibolero Trail flowed across the desert. Hour after hour he rode under the burning sun, slowed by the shambling pace of the weary, overladen mules, near exhaustion himself, but grimly hanging on to finish the chore.

Long after full dark had fallen, Jim Hatfield, reeling with fatigue, rode down Cibolero's main street, his worn out mules shambling along behind him. At the sheriff's office, he drew rein. A light burned within. Slumping from the saddle, he stumbled up the steps and shoved open the door.

Sheriff White was seated with his boots on his desk, glowering into space. The boots came to the floor with a thud as Hatfield entered. The sheriff leaped to his feet.

"Hatfield!" he exclaimed. "Where in blazes did yuh come from? What happened? Tell me—"

Hatfield waved a weary hand. "Wait," he said. "I'll tell you all about it later. Right now I want just three things. First, did you bring my horse in okay? Yes? Fine! Second, I want you to go out and take charge of that damn silver and feed the mules that packed it here. Third, I want a bed. I haven't had three hours of sleep in three nights."

The sheriff stared at the Lone Wolf's lined, haggard face and bloodshot eyes. He jerked his thumb toward the door of the inner room.

"The bed's in there," he said. "Tumble into it. I'll be settin' beside it when yuh wake up. And then I want somethin'. I want to know—how in hell did yuh do it!"

6

❖❖❖❖❖❖❖❖

SHERIFF WHITE was as good as his word. When Hatfield awoke, late the following morning, he was sitting beside the bed, smoking.

"Just come in from feedin' crow to some gents," he remarked.

"How's that?" Hatfield asked.

"Well," said the sheriff, "it was like this. We follered yuh as I told yuh we would, but, as yuh learned, it's a long amble around the hills to where the crik comes out. We found the boat, all right, but neither hide nor hair of you or the silver bricks. We nosed around and found where a lot of horses had been tied, but that was all. We was plumb flabbergasted—didn't know what to think. After a while we gave up, and headed back to town. It was past daylight when we finally got in and told what had happened. Then the talkin' commenced. Steve Tule, a nice feller and a good friend of mine, started the ball rollin' without meanin' to, I reckon. He wondered out loud just who you were and where yuh come from. All of a sudden folks was lookin' sideways at each other. A jigger piped up with, 'a hundred and fifty thousand dollars is a heap of money.' Finally somebody come right out with the opinion that you were in cahoots with the outfit, or some other one of like sort, and had hightailed with the silver bricks. I wouldn't believe it, and Cas Klingman 'lowed to whup the socks off some jiggers if they didn't latigo their jaws. But the talk went on, fast and furious, with folks linin' up and takin' sides. The upshot of the matter was the manager of the Monarch Mine swore out a warrant for yore arrest and offered a reward for yuh. I'd ought to have collected that reward when I roused him out of bed last night. We could have split it between us. Talks different this mornin'. The fellers what was cussin' you out yesterday are talkin' loudest for yuh today. Reckon that's the way with folks, though. Funny, nobody happen to hit on what really happened, though it shouldn't have been hard to figger out, if we'd just used our heads a mite."

"That's where I slipped, too," Hatfield said thoughtfully. "I was so busy getting through those infernal canyons that I never took time to figger somebody would be sure to be waiting somewhere downstream for the boat to show up. I ambled right up to the hellions and got a loop dropped on me."

"Just what did happen?" the sheriff asked expectantly.

Hatfield told him, in detail. The sheriff swore luridly, and wagged his head admiringly.

"Yuh're shore quite a feller, Jim," he declared. "What did yuh use to get them hinges loose?"

"Oh, a little chunk of metal I had on me," Hatfield evaded. "It was a hard tussle, but it finally worked out.

"What I'd like to know," he added thoughtfully, "is where that bunch holed up during the time between the robbery at Klingman's ranch and when they tackled the silver carts. They sure didn't go south to the Rio Grande after grabbing off Klingman's money, and they didn't head for that cabin, either. They stayed right in the section, somewhere."

"Yuh figger it was the same bunch?" the sheriff exclaimed excitedly.

Hatfield shrugged his shoulders. "Well, it doesn't stand

to reason that two outfits of a dozen or so each are operating in the same section, does it?" he countered.

"Hardly," the sheriff admitted. "Hell knows I hope not.
One is more'n plenty. Well, anyhow, they didn't hang
onto the silver, and we thinned 'em out by four, includin'
the one you did for in the cabin. That's a start, anyhow.
Klingman told me yuh signed up to ride for him. Mighty
glad to hear it. I've a notion I'll have use for yuh, too,
befcre this business is hogtied. Hope yuh won't mind
if I call on yuh."

"Be glad to lend a hand any time I can," Hatfield assured him.

The sheriff nodded with satisfaction. "Yuh had ought
to be a peace officer, son," he said. "Yuh got all the ear
marks of a good one. We'll have a talk about that later,
if yuh decide to coil yore twine in the section. Now, I
reckon yuh could stand a mite of breakfast. I've been too
busy myself to eat yet. Get yore clothes on and we'll amble over to the Busted Flush for a s'roundin'. Cas Klingman rode back to his spread last night, but he'll be in
town later. Reckon yuh'll want to wait for him."

Together they repaired to the Busted Flush. Upon en-
tering the saloon, Hatfield observed Steve Tule standing near the end of the bar. He stood with his feet wide
apart, erect and soldierly in bearing, one hand resting on
his hip, his eyes gazing into space and apparently deep
in thought. His face was slightly haggard and he looked
tired.

Hatfield's black brows drew together. There was again
something elusively familiar about the man, especially in
his present pose.

"Now where *have* I seen that jigger before, or somebody that looks almighty like him?" the Ranger asked
himself.

Tule turned his head, his glance rested on the new
arrivals and he waved a cordial greeting.

"Glad you came out of that ruckus okay, Hatfield," he called in his pleasantly modulated voice. "White told me about it. You did a fine job, all right."

Hatfield and White returned the greeting and passed to a nearby table. Together they had a satisfactory meal and both felt much better in consequence. When, a little later, they left the saloon, Steve Tule was still standing at the end of the bar, gazing moodily into space.

As they walked slowly up the street, they met big *Don* Ramon Garcia, the owner of the Cross G ranch. Garcia nodded shortly to the sheriff. He glanced keenly at Hatfield, a speculative gleam in his eyes, half hesitated, as if inclined to speak, then passed on. The sheriff noted the byplay.

"Garcia looked at yuh almost like he knowed yuh," the peace officer observed. "Thought for a minute he was goin' to stop. You ever meet him before?"

"Not that I know of," Hatfield returned, a thoughtful expression on his face. "No, not that I know of. How long has he been in this section?"

"Little more than a year," White returned. "Come here and bought the Cross G from old Thankful Yates, who had let it purty well run to seed. He's a good cowman, Garcia, but he doesn't get along with folks over well. Seems to have a reg'lar gift of rubbin' folks the wrong way. Captain Ben Wallace is about the only jigger in the section he's pertickler friendly with, but Captain Ben sort of favors oilers. Says they're misunderstood and if they have a chance their country will be different. He's always sayin' if old Sam Houston had lived and put his grand plan over, *manana* land would be handled just as well and be doin' just as good as America."

"He's got something there," Hatfield replied thoughtfully, "but it'll take time, and the right man. The man will come, sooner or later, though. You and I may not live to see it, but it'll come."

"Mebbe," White admitted dubiously, "but there ain't many signs of it right now. The country down south is in one hell of a mess, a plumb trouble spot, and the trouble keeps spillin' over the River for us to handle," he added morosely.

They returned to the sheriff's office for a smoke and a gabfest. An hour or so later Caswell Klingman rode in. He greeted Hatfield with the utmost enthusiasm.

"I'll have plenty to say to certain gents who were busy shootin' their big mouths off yesterday," he declared with intense satisfaction.

"How's things down at the spread?" asked White.

"We cleaned up the mess and are gettin' ready to build," Klingman replied. His brows drew together in thought.

"I sure wish there was somebody hereabouts who understands masonry and stone handlin'," he remarked. "If there was, I'd build a stone *casa* that wouldn't burn down, no matter what happened.

"Captain Ben Wallace has an old quarry on his place, and stacks and stacks of blocks of cut stone that's been layin' there for years," he explained to Hatfield. "I've a notion I could buy them rocks from Captain Ben, cheap. I'd build with 'em if I knew how to handle 'em. The boys are purty handy with tools of any kind, but they ain't familiar with stone work and, the chances are, would botch the job."

Hatfield looked thoughtful a moment, apparently arrived at some decision.

"If you can get the stone, I've a notion I can line up the boys on how to handle it," he remarked.

"Yuh mean it?" Klingman exclaimed, his eyes brightening. "Yuh sure?"

"I'm sure," Hatfield returned quietly. "You get the stone and I'll see to the laying of it."

"By gosh, I'll take yuh up on it!" Klingman declared.

"What yuh say—we ride up to Captain Ben's place right now?"

"Okay by me," Hatfield replied, getting to his feet. "Where'd you say you put up my horse, Sheriff?"

After some five miles of riding in a northeasterly direction, Hatfield and Klingman neared the spacious ranchhouse of the old adventurer, soldier of fortune, and cattle baron, Captain Ben Wallace. The old fighter himself met them at the door with a hospitable bellow.

"Come in! come in!" he shouted. "Mighty glad to see yuh, Cas. Glad to see yore friend, too. Hatfield? Glad to know yuh, Hatfield. Light off and squat."

They entered the big living room, which was furnished with elegance and taste. Almost instantly, Hatfield's attention was held by a full-length painting, life size, that dominated the far wall.

It was the portrait of a man—a tall, broad-shouldered, strikingly handsome man whose piercing eyes seemed to look into the distance and see splendid visions. His apparel was rich, vivid with color. His right hand rested on the hilt of the sword that hung from his hip.

Hatfield stared. His lips pursed in a soundless whistle.

"So that's it!" he muttered. "That's where I saw that jigger. I rec'lect this painting—what I saw was a copy, the chances are. Hernán Cortes, conquistador, Governor of New Spain. And Steve Tule is the spittin' image of him! If this doesn't beat all: a jigger who talks like a New Englander looking so much like Cortes he might be his son. Of all the queer things!"

Old Ben Wallace noted the direction of Hatfield's gaze.

"Like my painting?" he asked, a note of pride in his voice. "A portrait of Hernán Cortes, painted by Mantegna, the great artist of the Paduan School. Said to be the only portrait he ever did. They say he painted it when he was an old man. I got it down in Mexico

City, cost me plenty, but worth the price. Cortes was really a great man, a man of vision. If his notions had been followed by those who came after him, the Mexico of today would be a different country. He died too soon. Great men always die too soon, like Cortes, and Lincoln, and General Sam Houston. But they live on, in others."

"And their mistakes also sometimes live on—in others," Hatfield said gravely.

Wallace stared. A retort seemed rising to his lips. But there was something about this tall young man with the sternly handsome face and assured manner that gave pause even to Ben Wallace.

"Mebbe," he admitted reflectively. "Never thought of it that way before. Mebbe yuh're right, son. Know anythin' about paintin'?"

"A little," Hatfield admitted. "Enough to be able to appreciate such a work as that, anyhow."

A pleased smile crossed Ben Wallace's rugged face.

"And able, too, to appreciate the good great men try to accomplish—perhaps?" he suggested.

"Perhaps," Hatfield agreed, smiling slightly, his steady green eyes resting on the old man's face. Wallace, tall as he was, had to look up a trifle to meet them.

For some reason, not apparent, Ben Wallace seemed to find that steady gaze a trifle disconcerting. He grunted, cleared his throat, glanced away, and abruptly changed the subject.

"What brings yuh up here, Cas?" he asked of Klingman. "Just a sociable visit, or is there something I can do for yuh?"

Klingman outlined the object of his visit. Wallace nodded his big head.

"Sure yuh can have 'em," he said. "Cheap, too. I been wonderin' what to do with them rocks for a long time. The old jigger who owned this spread when I bought it had somethin' in mind for 'em—he quarried 'em—I don't know just what. They'll make a fine *casa*, all right, if they're put together right."

"Hatfield 'lows he knows how to put 'em together," explained Klingman.

Ben Wallace shot the Lone Wolf a keen glance, but forbore asking questions.

After a satisfactory arrangement had been arrived at, relative to the building stone, Hatfield and Klingman enjoyed an excellent meal with Wallace and departed, for it was getting late. As they ambled along the trail to town they saw a man riding at great speed across the prairie in the direction of the Forked Five ranchhouse. Klingman frowned as he recognized *Don* Ramon Garcia.

"What's that yaller-haired hellion in such a hurry to see old Ben about?" he wondered. "Mark my word on it, somethin' will happen before long. It always does when that jigger goes sashayin' around like that. Trouble follers him like buzzards."

As they rode into Cibolero, Klingman glanced at the westwardly sun.

"We might as well spend the night in town," he decided. "I want to make arrangements for havin' them rocks hauled down to the spread."

Klingman contacted a man who did freight hauling from Como to Cibolero and contracted the transportation of the stone from Wallace's ranch. Then he and Hatfield repaired to the Busted Flush for supper. While they were eating, *Don* Ramon Garcia entered, glanced around the room and then occupied a nearby table. Several times Hatfield sensed the Spaniard's gaze upon him. Once he intercepted Garcia's intensely speculative look. Garcia glanced away quickly, however, and went on eating. Before he had finished a man entered and approached his table, a lithe Mexican who glided noiselessly across the room and muttered a few words of Spanish. Garcia replied in the same language, and the Mexican, with a quick, furtive glance that embraced the entire room, departed as silently as he had come. A little later, Garcia also left the room.

Hatfield and Klingman had a couple of drinks together, talked for a while and then decided to go to bed.

"I arranged with old Brad, the stable keeper, for a couple of rooms he has over the stalls," Klingman said. "They're clean, and it's quieter there than at the Cowman's Hotel, where the boys are always raisin' hell at all hours of the night."

"I like to sleep close to my horse," Hatfield agreed.

They adjourned to the stable, which sat on an alley off the main street. In answer to Klingman's hammering on the door, a bolt was shot and a gruff voice bade them enter. Klingman glanced in surprise at the man who had admitted them. It was not the bearded old stable keeper but a dark-faced individual with beady black eyes.

"Brad is out for a spell and left me in charge," he remarked as he closed the door. "I been workin' for him for a few days. He said to ask you gents if there was anythin' yuh wanted before yuh hit the hay."

"We'll take a look at the cayuses, and then I reckon that's all," Klingman replied.

The horses were found to be properly cared for and all their wants supplied. Klingman and Hatfield ascended the stairs to the little rooms partitioned off from the big haymow.

"I'm dog tired," the rancher observed. "No sleep night before last and mighty little last night. I feel the need of a good session of ear poundin'. See yuh in the mornin'."

Hatfield said goodnight and entered his own room. It was simply furnished but clean. Having slept late, he was still very much awake. He hesitated a moment, then drew a chair to the window and sat down. He rolled a cigarette and smoked thoughtfully, pondering the events of the past few days.

"Sure got off to a flying start in this section," he mused. "One thing right after another. Wonder what's next in line. Something big is building up here, or I'm a heap mistaken. Wonder who's the big skookum he-wolf of the pack who's directing things. Ben Wallace has all the earmarks, but somehow I can't figger that old jigger going in for robbery and murder. Like so many of his kind, he figgers he's a law to himself, but with limits. No, I can't see it. There's somebody else hereabouts who doesn't stop at anything. The question is, who? And I still don't know a bit more than when I started about the smuggling. That stuff is coming north is sure for certain, but according to the Customs folks, no goods are showing up south of the Line. Which is plumb unusual."

All of a sudden he straightened in his chair, struck by a sudden thought.

"Those rifles I saw in the cabin!" he muttered. "I wonder now? Could the goods coming north be bartered for guns of the latest and best make? They would be easy to transport, and they wouldn't be apt to show up in the general markets. But who in blazes would be going in for guns in big numbers. No particular profit in guns. They can be gotten without much trouble, and the duty on them is not heavy enough to make smuggling worth while. No, that isn't the answer, or wouldn't seem to be. I reckon the ones I saw were just for the use of that owl-hoot bunch; but then again, a bunch like that is always well fixed for irons. The one in the saddle boot of the horse I rode to town was a good one, and not one of the sort I saw in the cabin. The whole business is sure a puzzler."

He finished his cigarette and pinched out the butt, but still he sat by the window, thinking. *Don* Ramon Garcia's rugged face floated up in his memory.

"That jigger sure acts as if he knows me, or thinks he does," he mused. "Wonder if he does? But if he's mixed up in something and has spotted me for a Ranger, he'd hardly let on. His game would be to pass me up without a second look, and he always acts like he was on the verge of speaking to me. Wonder if he could be the jigger directing things up here? One thing is sure for certain, the sheriff and Cas Klingman have some such notion. He appears to be on good terms with Wallace, too. Wonder if that pair have something up their sleeves? If they have, what is it?"

The question was a poser. Hatfield considered it from all angles, and could arrive at no satisfactory conclusion. He shook his head, staring out the black square of the open window.

The night was very dark, with a hush in the air that hinted at rain. From the main street came the subdued murmur of the town's night activities; but the stable seemed to rest in a pool of silence.

So intense was the stillness, that what sounded like the faint creaking of one of the stair steps brought Hatfield's head around with a jerk. The sound was not repeated, however, and he concluded that it was doubtless a movement on the part of one of the horses downstairs, or a rat under the floor boards. He turned back to the window, still thinking deeply. Then a second sound brought his head around more quickly than before—a faint creaking in the direction of the door. As he stared across the room, a narrow slit of dusky gray suddenly split the black darkness that swathed the opposite wall. For a moment Hatfield was at a loss as to what it could be. Then he recalled that a lighted lantern hung on a peg at the foot of the stairs. A little of the light from it seeped to the upper wall. What he saw was that light, struggling through the crack of the slightly opened door.

As he stared, the bar of gray widened, inch by crawling inch.

The Lone Wolf was not given to nervousness; but just the same he felt the palms of his hands grow slightly moist. There was something indescribably menacing in that slow, stealthily opening door. Tense and alert, he continued to gaze across the room, hardly daring to breathe.

The door opened still more. A shadow loomed against the faint glow in the hall. It took shape and form. The door opened wider and the shadow moved forward. Hatfield could just make out its shape as it stole across the room toward the bed and bent over. Abruptly it straightened up, with a muttered curse, and whirled toward the window.

Hatfield went sideways out of his chair as his eye caught the gleam of shifted metal. Something hissed through the air and thudded against the chair back. Hatfield jerked his gun and fired two shots at the crouching shadow, the reports blending into one. Echoing the crash of his gun came a strangled cry, a solid thud as of a falling body, then a strange rapid tapping, as of boot heels beating a tattoo on the floor boards. He heard the thump of Klingman's feet in the next room, and his aroused bellow.

"Keep in the clear!" he shouted as the rancher's door banged open. He rolled sideways as he spoke, his gun jutting forward; but nothing happened. The beating of heels on the boards had ceased. The room was deathly silent.

Caswell Klingman was bawling questions in the hall. Hatfield got lithely to his feet.

"Hold it till I strike a light," he shouted back. He fumbled a match, lit it. The tiny flame flared up and revealed the sprawled body of a man on the floor beside the bed.

"Get that lantern from downstairs and bring it here," Hatfield called to Klingman. The thud of the rancher's bare feet sounded on the steps. A moment later he came puffing back, holding high the lighted lantern.

"What the hell's goin' on?" he bawled.

"Don't know for sure," Hatfield replied, "but by the looks of that knife struck in the back of the chair, I'd say somebody meant business."

Klingman swore luridly as he glared at the long blade driven deeply in the wooden chair back. He held the lantern to the figure on the floor, peered into its distorted face.

"It's the hellion who let us in," he exclaimed. "What *is* this all about?"

Hatfield was struck by a sudden thought.

"Old Brad, the stable keeper!" he exclaimed. "He sleeps downstairs, in the back, doesn't he? Come on, bring the lantern."

He swiftly led the way downstairs and to the back of the building, to where a closed door indicated the location of the keeper's living quarters. He flung the door open. Klingman held the lantern high.

Across the room a bunk was built against the wall. On it lay a figure that writhed and strained and made muttering, unintelligible sounds. It was the old stable keeper. He was bound and gagged. His face was covered with dried blood that had flowed from a gash in the side of his grizzled head.

Hatfield quickly jerked the gag from the old man's mouth and cut his bonds. He sat up, sputtering and cursing, and dabbing at his injury.

"I was just openin' the door when somebody bent a gun barrel over my head," he replied to their questions. "The next thing I knowed, I was in here hawgtied. Happened just after dark. No notion how long I've been here. What the hell is it all about? Horses gone?"

"They're safe," Hatfield replied. He was about to explain the happenings in his room when a loud knocking sounded at the outer door.

"Careful, Jim, get yore gun ready," cautioned Kling-man. "No use takin' any chances; no tellin' who that may be."

Hatfield nodded. He strode to the outer door, his right hand swinging close to his hip. Standing well to one side, he unlocked the door and flung it open. A man strode in, glancing keenly about. It was *Don* Ramon Garcia!

7

GARCIA GLANCED keenly about, his hand on the butt of his gun.

"I was passing and I heard a shot in here, and somebody yelling," he explained. "Thought I'd better find out what was going on."

He cast an interrogatory glance at Hatfield and Klingman. The former recounted the recent happenings in a few terse sentences. Garcia shook his handsome head.

"Seems nobody is safe hereabouts of late," he remarked, his precise English flavored by the merest trace of accent. "Looks like saving that shipment for the Monarch people is causing you trouble," he added with a significant glance at Hatfield.

The Lone Wolf nodded without comment. Cas Klingman growled something under his mustache. A querulous bellow from the back room returned them to the injured stable keeper. Hatfield examined his wound.

"No particular damage done," was his verdict. "We'll rouse out Doc McChesney and send him over to patch you up. No, let's have a look at that jigger upstairs."

They repaired to Hatfield's room and gave the dead knife wielder a careful once-over. He was an unsavory looking specimen, viewed at close range, his lips drawn back over yellow, nicked teeth.

"Reg'lation Border scum," growled Klingman. "Ever see him before, Garcia? I ain't."

74

"Yes, I have," *Don* Ramon replied slowly. "I'm sure it is a man I saw drinking in the Busted Flush saloon this afternoon. He was by himself. Looked like a hard character. I've a notion Steve Tule thought so, too. Anyhow, after watching him for a while, he walked up to him and said a word or two to him. The feller glowered at him, mumbled something and slouched out. I don't recall ever seeing him before today."

Hatfield nodded. Klingman snorted under his mustache.

"I suppose the sheriff should be notified," remarked Hatfield. "He'll want to make some disposition of the body."

"I'll go get White, and Doctor McChesney," *Don* Ramon volunteered. "White was in his office when I passed by."

He hurried down the stairs. Klingman scowled after his departing back.

"Didn't I tell yuh that hellion is always around when somethin' busts loose," he said. "Yuh'd think he was hangin' around waitin'. Now what was he doin' up this alley at this time of night?"

Hatfield said nothing, but the furrow of concentration deepened between his black brows, a sign the Lone Wolf was doing some hard thinking. He began to turn out the dead man's pockets, discovering nothing that interested him except a well filled tobacco pouch. He opened the pouch and sniffed the contents, his eyes thoughtful. He tightened the pucker strings and slipped the pouch in his pocket.

"I'll keep this as a souvenir," he observed.

"Everybody to his taste," grunted Klingman. "I knowed a jigger who packed stuffed rattlesnakes around with him. Another kept a dried ear of a feller he shot, in his vest pocket."

The dead man's knife, driven so deeply into the chair

back that Hatfield had to tug hard to remove it, was a peculiar appearing weapon, thick and heavy of blade, short of handle.

"A throwing knife, home-made affair ground out from a file," he decided.

He studied the blade, his brows drawing together.

"Brand new file," he mused. "You can still make out the maker's name, up close to the handle."

The furrow of concentration deepened still more between his brows, and into his strangely colored eyes came a slight glow.

"Wicked lookin' thing," observed Klingman. His face became grave.

"They're after yuh, son," he said. "Those hellions ain't goin' to forget losin' that silver. I hate to say it, but I've a notion the best thing you can do is fork that yaller horse and ride out of this section pronto."

"Good advice," agreed Hatfield, "I'm not taking it."

"Didn't figger yuh would," admitted Klingman, "but I still figger yuh'd ought to. It's a bad bunch and will stop at nothin'. Wish this hellion had lived long enough to talk some. Might have given us a line on who's at the head of this skullduggery."

"He may have given us a line, anyhow," Hatfield replied.

Klingman gave him a curious look, but Hatfield did not see fit to elaborate on the remark.

A few minutes later *Don* Ramon and the sheriff hurried up the stairs. White swore disgustedly, and glowered at the dead knife wielder.

"If yuh'd been asleep, yuh would have got that sticker between yore ribs," the sheriff growled. "Son, I'm scairt yuh're on a spot. Those hellions won't never let up till they get yuh."

"Mebbe," Hatfield admitted noncommittally. "Ever see this one before, Sheriff?"

White shook his head. "And I'm glad I won't ever see him again," he answered vindictively. "Well, we're whittlin' 'em down. At this rate they soon won't have enough to operate with."

"They'll always get enough, so long as the head of the outfit is maverickin' around," Hatfield declared with conviction. "I've a notion, too, that we'll soon hear from them again. It takes plenty of dinero to keep an outfit like this going, and I've a notion the loss of the silver they counted on put a crimp in their plans. They'll strike again soon. Keep yore eyes open, Sheriff.

"I will," White returned with emphasis.

"Anything that would afford a big haul," Hatfield said. "Payrolls, railroad shipments, cattle. They'll all bear watching."

"That last reminds me," said Klingman. "Just as soon as we get the new *casa* going good, we've got to get a shipping herd together. I'm going to be sort of pushed for cash money, come the first of the month. Plenty of fat beefs ready for market on the spread, though, and the market is good right now. We'll start work on 'em in another week or so."

The sheriff had dispatched a deputy to rout out Doc McChesney, who was also coroner. He arrived at this juncture, gave the dead owlhoot a once-over and replied to a question from Hatfield.

"Nope, yuh don't need to be here for the inquest. I'll take yore deposition right now. The sheriff and me will take care of everything tomorrow. Now I'll tie up Brad's head."

After the doctor had finished with him, the old stable keeper stumped up the stairs with a bucket and mop.

"If you gents will pack this hellion downstairs, I'll clean up a bit and then we'll all go to bed," he suggested.

"Good notion," agreed Klingman. Hatfield and me want to get to work on our buildin' job tomorrow. The

first loads of rock should be delivered by early afternoon."

The following day, the hauling contractor was as
good as his word and the work on the *casa* began. A
week later, Caswell Klingman gazed at the well planned
foundations and ground works, and the rising walls, of
his new ranchhouse and shook his head in wordless ad-
miration.

"Hatfield," he asked at length, "where in blazes did
yuh learn so much about buildin'?"

Jim Hatfield, who before the murder of his father by
wideloopers had sent him into the Rangers, had had three
years in a famous college of engineering, smiled slightly.

"Oh, I've helped build a house or two," he evaded.

"Yeah?" Klingman returned dryly. "I'd a notion yuh
helped build a town or two!"

Hatfield contemplated the building.

"Brown and Mason are first rate carpenters," he observed. "If it's okay with you, we'll leave them to the
wood work and get busy on that shipping herd."

"That's a notion," replied Klingman. "That herd is
mighty important about now. You and me are doin'
purty well bunkin' in the barn, and I reckon we can stand
it a spell longer. We'll start work on the herd tomorrow.
I figger the south range is our best bet. Lots of cool, grass-
grown canyons in the hills down there. The critters hole
up in them gorges durin' the hot weather. Sort of a hard
range to work—considerable of a chore, combin' the
beefs out of them holes and brakes—but it'll pay. Okay,
I'll line the boys up."

Work on the shipping herd started the following morning. As Klingman predicted, plenty of beefs were found
in the canyons and brakes, but it was no easy task to
round them up. The work was done with deliberation,
for the cows were heavy in flesh and fat. The cowboys
divided in small parties, which scattered until the

riders were well separated. Klingman sent word to the adjoining ranches and each assigned a certain number of hands to augment the Tumbling K outfit and cut out animals wearing their respective brands, of which there were considerable numbers, for the animals drifted a good deal at this time of the year. Taking care of this chore when such an opportunity presented itself would lighten the work of the regular fall roundup, which was not far off, and which would be taken part in by all the spreads, for the whole valley was open range.

The cows, combed out in ones and twos and small groups, were driven to a designated holding spot where the work of cutting out would be done. Here the cattle were held in close herd, a compact group kept in place by picked riders assigned to the task. When the roundup was finished, cowboys on nimble-footed horses would invade the herd and cut out the various brands.

As the work was pressing, for the first few days, Hatfield put a night drive into action. Small squads of riders, usually one or more from each outfit represented, were sent out ten or fifteen miles from the holding spot and very early in the morning began driving cattle in the country around designated for the next day. Before the Tumbling K herd was finally ready for the drive to the railroad, cut-backs and culls would be separated from the beef cut. All coulees, canyons, foothills, flats and draws were carefully combed for hiding cattle.

"I don't want any mavericks sashayin' around as proof of bad combin'," Klingman warned his hands.

Jim Hatfield had been selected as the roundup captain, and his word was law, not even an owner being allowed to contradict or countermand his orders.

Caswell Klingman, heeding Hatfield's warning, took no chances with the big herd that grew steadily day by day. He and Hatfield together selected the holding spot with an eye to a possible raid by the owlhoot band operating in the section. The herd was held and bedded in the mouth of a shallow canyon with perpendicular walls more than two hundred feet high. The canyon was a box and could be entered only by way of the mouth. Taking not the least chance, Hatfield thoroughly explored the canyon before taking up position in its mouth.

"I had a little experience with this sort of a crack, once," he told Klingman. "A herd was held in the mouth of a canyon just like this one. Nobody could get into it without passing the guard at the mouth. That was fine, but the roundup captain neglected to know for sure what was back in that canyon. As it happened, some enterprising gents with lose business notions holed up in the canyon the day before the herd was assembled there to hit the trail the following day. They waited until it was dark, then came skalley-hootin' out of the canyon, shot the night hawks and stampeded the herd. We don't want anything like that to happen."

"Yuh're darn right we don't," Klingman agreed heartily, and assisted in scouring the canyon, which, however, was found untenanted.

Seven picked riders, heavily armed, were assigned to guard the herd at all times, day and night, and Klingman and Hatfield rode back to the incompleted ranchhouse easy of mind the night before the final cutting out and the preparation of the Tumbling K cows for trailing.

"She's a lulu, and most of the critters are ours," Klingman said, turning in his saddle to gaze back at the great mass of cattle contentedly feeding in the canyon mouth. Farther back was a brush corral which held the horses of the hands assigned to guard duty. The guards themselves were comfortably camped under the overhang of the cliff. Their position could be stormed only from the front, and Hatfield and Klingman had no fear that wide-loopers would attempt such a suicidal foray. Outside the canyon mouth was open prairie on the east; but on the west was a long slope thickly grown with chaparral.

"We'll ride back here as soon as it is light tomorrow morning," said Klingman, glancing at the sunset blazing behind the western crags. "I'll be glad to get home tonight. I'm hungry and dog tired."

"It's been a hard chore," Hatfield agreed, settling himself in the saddle for the five-mile ride to the ranchhouse.

Meanwhile, the hands guarding the herd heeded the cook's strident bellow to "come and get it or I'll throw it away!" On the little shelf of open ground beneath the overhang they filled their plates and cups and began putting their food away with the appetite of long hours in the open. Clem Shore, who was in charge of the guard, glanced contentedly over the backs of the horses in the corral at the cows peacefully chewing their cuds a hundred yards or so farther down the canyon. His gaze ranged to the prairie beyond the canyon mouth and the silent, brush covered slope.

"Whitridge, Russell and Jasper will take first ridin' trick tonight," he directed. "Keep yore eyes open, and if yuh hear anythin' that don't sound just right, shoot first and ask questions afterward. Not that I figger anybody will be damn fool enough to try to snake them cows out of the canyon; but we ain't takin' no chances. The Boss would take our hides off and nail 'em to the bar door if anythin' happened to this herd. We—what in blazes!"

From the cliff top, two hundred feet above, something came hurtling, a dome-shaped object that spun through the air, landed in the horse corral with a crash and flew to a thousand fragments. As the amazed cowboys leaped to their feet, another followed it, and another, and another. Some struck within the brush corral, others landed among the startled cattle.

"Bee hives!" howled Bert Pierce, clapping his hands to his posterior portions in painful remembrance. "Somebody's chuckin' bee hives off the rimrock!"

Pierce was right. The objects crashing to the ground *were* beehives, and they weren't empty, either! From their smashed homes, swarmed thousands of the maddest bees in Texas, all itching for fight and ready to take it out on anything ready to hand. Almost instantly the frantic horses in the corral were spotted with the yellow demons. Nor did the cattle lack for attention.

The maddened horses leaped the corral and fled down canyon, trying to escape the countless stings that stabbed at their sensitive ears and other exposed parts. Into the milling herd they charged, kicking and biting.

At this onslaught, the cattle, already demoralized with fright and wild with pain, stampeded. In a solid mass of rolling eyes, clashing horns and thundering hoofs, they tore from the canyon mouth, the horses slashing their way through the herd and taking the lead.

"After them cayuses!" bawled Clem Shore.

The cowboys leaped from the shelf and headed down canyon, only to meet clouds of wrathful bees. Another second and they were in full flight *up* the canyon, yelling and cursing and slapping and thrashing. Into the brush they dived, where, in the already deepening shadows, their tormentors could not see to get at them. As they peered back at the swirling enemy, Beak Prescott let out a bellow of understanding.

"Look!" he whooped. "Look, comin' out of the brush!"

His cursing companions saw a dozen or so masked men riding out of the chaparral in the wake of the fleeing cattle. They swiftly overhauled the herd, spread around it, guiding, compacting.

"The rifles!" bawled Shore. "Get the rifles and line sights with the blankety-blank-blanks! They're wide-loopin' our cows!"

The punchers tried to obey orders; but the rifles were on the bench beneath the overhang, and between them and the spot were clouds of bees still looking for trouble, and ready to dish it out in large helpin's.

Three times the Tumbling K hands tried to reach the bench, and three times they were driven back. Faces were puffed, eyes were swollen almost shut.

"It's no use," wailed Shore. "We'll hafta hole up here in the brush till it gets dark and the hellions can't see us."

Not until full darkness had fallen, were they able to sneak from their retreat and start, limping along in their high-heeled boots, on the five mile tramp to the ranch-house.

8

OLD CASWELL KLINGMAN raved like a madman when hours later, Clem Shore told his story.

"Stampeding a herd with bees, that's a plumb new one," Hatfield remarked. "I got a look at those bees the day Pierce roped the hive. They're yellow Cyprians, the most excitable and meanest of all bees. That many of them, mad as they must have been after being packed all that distance in plugged up hives, would stampede a herd of elephants. All right, boys, get the rigs on your horses and we'll hightail after the hellions. They've got a long head start on us, but those cows are heavy and will slow them down. They'll go by way of the Smugglers' Trail, won't they, Cas?"

"That's right," said Klingman. "It's the only way out of the valley, down there, and it's a hard pull through the notch. We might have a chance, after all."

"Send a man to notify the sheriff," Hatfield suggested. "He can follow us with a posse. And have the jigger stop off at Andy Cahil's place and see what they did to him. They couldn't have taken those hives away in daylight without putting the old man out of commission first. It'll be lucky if he wasn't cashed in."

In a very short time the Tumbling K punchers, including even the swollen-faced, half-blind victims of the bees, were urging their horses up the slopes to the gray ribbon of the Smugglers' Trail. At a fast pace they headed south along the winding track. A few miles from where the trail climbed the slope to the notch, they found evidence of the passing of the herd.

"They're a long ways ahead of us, but mebbe we'll get a break of some kind," Hatfield said. "Sift sand, you work dodgers. We're not licked yet!"

Up the long slope and into the dark and crooked pass, they thundered, watchful, alert; but they found no trace of the wideloopers. Nor on the long slant that led down to the arid desolation of the desert which lay gray and ghostly in the starlight, seemingly as still and strange and alien to man as the silver spangled firmament above.

"They might turn off somewhere down here," Hatfield cautioned his companions. "We'll hafta slow up and watch the tracks. Hope the wind doesn't start blowing. If it does, it'll shift the sand and fill in the prints in a hurry."

"And if it comes on to blow bad, we'll have a good chance of stayin' out here for good," Klingman added grimly. "This is a bad place to get caught in a storm. Plenty of bones out here, and not all of 'em of cows or horses."

A very short time afterward, they had grisly proof of the truth of his words when they passed a round, whitish object glimmering faintly with phosphorescent light. A closer glance showed it to be a bleached and fleshless human skull.

They were far out on the desert when the rose and scarlet of the dawn flushed the eastern sky. A tremulous golden glow flowed over the great arid plain. Chimney rocks stood out stark and black. Cholla cactuses, stiff and erect, brandished crooked deformed arms like truculent devils. The ridges of sand were like the waves of an ocean frozen while in motion. There was a breathless hush in the heavy air that had a creamy feel to it. Far ahead, dim with distance, rose a range of craggy, brush covered hills. And even farther to the east were other hills, misty and unreal, with rounded crests and indistinct outlines.

"Them's the *Espantosas*, the Haunted Hills," said Klingman, observing the direction of Hatfield's gaze. "Folks say the *Espantosas* change form and move around, so that a man usin' them for landmarks gets plumb lost. They're right. The *Espantosas* are giant sand dunes, and they do change shape when the wind blows. From time to time they look plumb different."

Hatfield gazed toward the ghostly rises, his brows drawing together. The east was fiery red, now, the few clouds edged with an angry scarlet. The light strengthened, luridly rubescent, and as he gazed, from the rounded summits of the misty hills sprang great flaunting flags and banners, glowing in the crimson light like "garments rolled in blood," wavering, withdrawing, spreading wide and drawing thin and tenuous. He knew all too well what those weird streamers meant.

"Wind," he said to Klingman. "Wind stirring the sand on the tops of the dunes, and it's coming this way fast. I'm afraid we're in for trouble."

"And look there ahead!" Klingman exclaimed in excited tones.

Hatfield gazed, and nodded. Not far from the first slopes of the hills to the south he could just make out a number of moving specks.

"It's them," he said. "That's the herd down there, heading into the hills. If that infernal storm will just hold off, we'll catch them up. But if it breaks here like it's blowing over there to the east, those hellions are liable to have things their way."

Tense with anticipation, the punchers urged their horses to their utmost speed. With excited faces, they stared into the south, where the laboring cows had grown from specks to black dots drawing toward the shadowy outlines of the hills.

"We'll get 'em!" exulted Clem Shore. "Watch me even up for them blasted bee stings!"

But before they had covered another mile, the storm broke. The newly risen sun changed from fiery red to a deep, weird magenta color. The air was filled with rushing yellow shadows as the loose sand and dust sprang up from the desert's face. The sky was no longer visible. Clouds of flying sand rustled through the air, and grains of gravel that stung like shot. The intermittent blasts of the wind had a furnace quality about them. They were hot with the withering, strength-sapping heat of gas fed flame. The whole landscape would be obscured in sweeping, curling sheets of dust; then, as the wind dropped for the moment, the air would clear somewhat, close to the ground. But high in the air the yellow pall still tossed and writhed, with the ghastly sun, like a red-orange moon seen through haze, glaring down, its rays tossed back and flattened by the swirling curtain of the dust.

Handkerchiefs swathed about their mouths, hat brims pulled low, the cowboys bent their heads to the gale and rode doggedly hour after dragging hour. The horses' gait had slowed to a shambling walk. They coughed and snorted, and now and again whinnied plaintively as they forged ahead through the terrible abyss of flying yellow shadows, heat and dust. All about was a strange yellow twilight, formless, limitless, its numbing monotony broken only by the spectral sun glaring through the dust like a bloody eye. Long since the pursuers had given up hope of overtaking the owlhoots before they reached the comparative sanctuary of the hills. The twilight of changing shadow made sure sight at any considerable distance impossible, and the sweeping rush, the hollow roar and rising shriek of the wind blotted out all other sounds.

"We could pass within a hundred yards of 'em and never see 'em," croaked Klingman, through his muffling neckerchief.

"They'll make straight for the hills," Hatfield assured him. "They'll never turn off from the trail in this storm. They'd be done for in an hour if they did."

"And we'll be done for in another hour, if we don't make the hills, or this infernal storm don't blow itself out," panted Klingman.

Hatfield did not answer. He knew the rancher was right. The awful heat, the unbreatheable air, was sapping their strength. Already the horses were stumbling. In Hatfield's ears was a strange roaring, an echo to the hollow roar of the wind under the yellow pall of dust. Strange visions began dancing before his eyes. He was conscious that his tongue was swelling, seeking to force its way between his cracked lips. A terrible thirst was gnawing at his vitals. His blood seemed to be heated to the boiling point, his muscles turning to water. Grimly he bent his head and rode on. Gradually he dropped back until he was rearmost of the laboring troop. Quickly his foresight was justified. He sensed a dark shape straying to one side. One of the cowboys, almost delirious with heat and thirst, his sight blinded, had let his horse stumble from the trail.

Hatfield urged Goldy forward. He shot out a long arm, gripped the reeling cowboy's bridle and gradually got his horse back on the trail. Still gripping the bridle, he quickened Goldy's pace a trifle and closed up with the straggling line.

"Might as well have let him go, though," he muttered dully to himself. "He'd just have gotten it over a little sooner, that's all. Here! This won't do!"

He flung up his head, squared his shoulders, got a grip on himself. With stinging, bloodshot eyes he stared ahead. Was it imagination, or was the choking dust cloud thinning a trifle, although the wind was blowing stronger than ever? Abruptly he realized that his saddle had taken on a slight backward slant. He knew what that meant. They were climbing the first slope of the hills! His voice rang out, exultant, encouraging—

"Hang on, feller! Hang on! We're leaving the desert. We'll be in clear air soon."

Hoarse croaks of renewed hope answered him. The horses quickened their shambling pace. Now the dust cloud was visibly thinning. More distant objects began to take on form and substance. Gray lines of light wound through the yellow pall. The hills ahead appeared once more, veiled in lilac haze that brightened to rose tinted silver. The heat, while still blistering, had perceptibly lessened. The air was becoming breatheable. They rose higher on the slope, and the wind became clean. Glancing back, Hatfield could see the ghastly yellow shroud that hid the face of the desert. But now it was below them. The sun had changed to gold. The sky was blue. Great, brush covered slopes were rearing up on either side as they rode into a narrow defile with cool blue shadows in its depths. A little more and Hatfield saw a silvery gleam ahead.

"Water!" he gasped to his companions. "A crik over there. Don't let the horses drink too much, and take it easy yourselves. We made it!"

Ten minutes later, the cowboys, refreshed by long draughts of the cool water, their strength swiftly returning, were rolling cigarettes while giving the horses a breather.

"How long were we out there?" Klingman asked the Ranger.

Hatfield glanced at the sun. "About three hours, I'd say," he calculated.

"Three hours!" returned the cowman. "It figgered up more like three centuries!"

"When you're caught in a storm like that, you don't

figger time by hours and minutes, but by how long you manage to stay alive," Hatfield replied gravely.

A little later Hatfield pinched out his cigarette. "Let's go," he told his companions. "Those sidewinders missed most of the storm and they've got another lead on us, but the cows must be getting almighty tired by now. We've still got a chance to catch them up before they make the River. They're ahead of us, all right. The marks on the trail show that."

The punchers saw to their cinches, mounted, and rode forward again, Hatfield and Klingman in the van. The trail bored deeper and deeper into the hills, with the long slopes of the defile sweeping upward toward the distant blue skyline. They were grown thick with brush and stunted trees that waved and tossed in the wind that still blew strongly from the southeast. Hatfield estimated the distance to the gorge of the Rio Grande, and their chances of overtaking the herd before it forded the River. It would be touch and go, he decided. The sun was almost directly overhead, so they had a good many hours of daylight to count on.

"We've got to do it before dark," he told himself. "Once they get across the river and night shuts down, they'll give us the slip. Also, the chances are somebody is waiting for them down below the Line, and that may make more than we can handle."

He quickened Goldy's pace until his irons rang a drumroll of sound on the hard surface of the trail. The horses of his followers were hard put to keep up with the great sorrel.

The defile wound on, narrower, now, the slopes higher. The sun crossed the zenith and began slanting toward the west. Soon the gorge would be shadowy. From the marks left by the passing cattle, Hatfield knew they were gaining on the quarry. He peered ahead, but the defile turned and slanted so that at no time could he see any great distance.

Suddenly he sniffed sharply. A familiar smell had assailed his nostrils—the pungent tang of burning wood.

"Surely those hellions wouldn't take a chance on stopping to light a fire and cook!" he muttered.

Instinctively he raised his eyes to the skyline ahead. There seemed to be a slight haze smoldering along it. Even as he gazed, the haze deepened, became a thin gray cloud rolling swiftly northward on the wings of the wind. Another moment and it was a darkish smudge boiling up above the rimrock, swiftly thickening, increasing in volume.

Hatfield's voice rang out, hard, incisive—

"Hold it! Pull up! The hellions have set fire to the brush ahead!"

The group came to a jostling, swearing halt. Sitting their panting horses, the cowboys stared at the thickening cloud ahead.

"This won't do," Hatfield said quickly. "That fire's coming this way fast. We've got to get out of here before we're trapped."

A wild yell from one of the cowboys answered him—

"We're trapped already! Look, the smoke's bilin' up behind us!"

Hatfield whirled in his saddle, his eyes narrowing, his face setting in granite lines. What the puncher said was true. A dense cloud was rising from the depths of the gorge in their rear. The fire there was undoubtedly burning close to the canyon floor.

For a moment there was near panic. Hatfield's voice, cool, incisive, stilled the tumult.

"We'll have to make it up the slope, that's all," he said. "They've fired the brush in front and behind. Must have left a hellion holed up back there waiting till we passed. Then when he saw the smoke rising ahead, he lit the brush in behind us. Nice bunch of sidewinders, all right. Okay, up the slope to the left here. It'll be hard going and no time to waste, but mebbe we can make it."

"The slope to the right is easier," Klingman pointed out.

"Yes," Hatfield agreed grimly, "and the chances are they'll figger us to take that, because it *is* easier. And just as liable as not, we'll run smack into a bunch of jiggers holed up on the rimrock, all set to blow us down. We go to the left."

"Yuh're liable to have somethin' there," Klingman admitted.

"Let's go," Hatfield said. "String out in single file, so as to be all set to help anybody whose horse might go down. If shooting starts, don't pay any attention to it, but keep going. The fire's the thing we've got to beat; it's deadlier than lead."

Into the brush they urged their nervous horses. The intelligent animals sensed that something was very wrong. They snorted, tossed their heads, rolled their eyes and blew through flaring nostrils, and tackled the slope with a will.

It was hard going. The brush was thick and retarded their progress. Stones rolled under their irons. There was loose shale and spaces of slippery earth. From the south dense clouds of smoke were rolling before the fierce wind. Soon there were sparks and whirling brands. Before they were halfway up the slope they could hear the roar and crackle of the flames rushing through the tinder-dry brush. The heat became oppressive, the air almost unbreatheable. Clouds of ash sifted down, causing men and horses to cough and gasp.

Some two-thirds of the way up the brush thinned. As the lead horses flashed onto the almost open space, something whined through the air overhead and smacked against a stone.

"The hellions are on the rimrock of the east slope—they're gettin' our range," Klingman called back to Hatfield.

The Lone Wolf nodded. His eyes were coldly gray, his lean face hard set.

"Keep going," he called to the rancher. Another moment and he had slipped from his saddle, slid his rifle from the boot and backed into the shadow of a shelf of stone.

Puffs of smoke were mushrooming up from the distant rimrock across the gorge. Slugs were whining all around him, but the swirling smoke made accurate shooting difficult. Hatfield threw the rifle to his shoulder, his eyes glinted along the sights. The rifle rang loudly, smoke spurted from its muzzle.

Back and forth he raked the rimrock with lead, until the hammer clicked on an empty shell. As he began slipping in fresh cartridges, a clump of brush tufting the distant rim was violently agitated. Something black pitched from it and rolled and bounded down the slope, vanishing at last into the growth.

"Got one of them," Hatfield muttered, with grim satisfaction. He emptied another magazine at the rim. The smoke puffs no longer arose across the misty gorge. Apparently the owlhoots had had enough of it, for the moment at least.

Far up the slope, old Cas Klingman let out a stentorian bellow.

"Come along, Jim," he whooped. "The fire's gettin' almighty close."

Glancing diagonally along the sag, Hatfield could see the wall of flame racing out of the south. He slid the rifle back into the boot, mounted and sent Goldy charging up the slope. The air was thick with ash and sparks and whirling brands. The waves of smoke restricted his vision to a few yards. He muffled his nose and mouth in his neckerchief, ducked his head low and urged the straining horse to greater speed. Goldy screamed as a reaching tongue of flame licked his hocks. He bounded forward, snorting and blowing, and into a wall of flame. Hatfield gasped with the unbearable heat. He felt the sting of the fire against his face. In his ears was a mighty roaring. He buried his face in Goldy's mane and grimly held on. Reeling in his saddle, he twined his fingers in the coarse hair of the mane and held on with a death grip. The fire roared about him. Flames singed his hair, his eyebrows. The smoke was a stifling cloud, thick with ash, sprinkled with stinging sparks.

Then abruptly he was in comparatively clear air once more. Behind him the fire boomed and crackled. Ahead the growth was thinning, to end in several hundred steep yards of naked stone and earth that swelled to the beetling rimrock.

Old Caswell Klingman, far up the slope, let out a bellow of relief as Hatfield shot into view from the wall of smoke and flame. The Tumbling K punchers, already clustered on the rimrock, cheered lustily. Goldy went scrambling upward, overtook the waiting Klingman. Together they toiled up the last few yards and gained the rim. Below them the fire bellowed angrily as it swept northward before the wind. The smoke was so thick now that the eastern rim was invisible.

With very little to say, the scorched troop rode along the rim in the murky light of the smoke veiled sun. The depths of the gorge were a welter of flame and smoke, but the wind booming across the rim cleared the upper air.

For several miles they rode, finally pausing on the lip of a long slope that tumbled steeply downward to level ground. In the distance to the south they could see the gorge of the Rio Grande. Of the rustled herd and the wideloopers there was no trace.

"They made it to the River, all right," Hatfield said. "Must have left part of their outfit behind to set the fire and hold us back. The rest shoved the cows along. They're in Mexico by now."

"Well, reckon that ends it," Klingman replied gloomily. He swept the terrain with an embracing glance.

"By circlin' to the west, I figger we can get through the hills and back to the trail," he remarked. "Reckon we might as well be headin' for home."

But Jim Hatfield, his eyes hard, his face bleak, turned Goldy's nose to the south.

"What yuh up to, Jim?" Klingman asked, wonderingly.

"I'm after that herd," Hatfield replied. "I don't intend to let those hellions get away with it. I know the country across the River. About twenty miles to the south, along a trail that must be the Smugglers' after it gets to the other side, is a town—Rosita. I happen to know it is a sort of clearing spot for smugglers and the like. The chances are mighty in favor of the bunch we trailed running those cows to Rosita, where they can dispose of them. I intend to find out. I know some folks in Rosita who may lend us a hand."

"Well," said Klingman with decision, "if yuh're headin' south, so am I, and the rest of the boys, if they've a mind to. Anyhow, I'm ridin' with yuh."

There was a general and determined assent from the rest of the outfit. But Hatfield shook his head.

"A big bunch like this would attract too much attention," he said. "Three or four men riding in from the north won't be particularly noticed. If you're set on going, Cas, okay. Then two more men will be enough. How about you, Shore, and you, Prescott. Ready to take a chance? It's liable to be a salty chore."

"I still want to even up for them damn bee stings," said Clem Shore, his scorched whiskers bristling on his angry face.

"Well, what we waitin' for?" growled the big-nosed Prescott.

Hatfield grinned slightly. "Okay, then," he said. "We'll head south. The rest of you jiggers make it back to the spread. Work to do up there. You might as well start another shipping herd, just in case we don't have any luck down below."

"And Lawyer Blaine at Como has my will in his safe," Klingman added significantly. "I ain't got no kin folks, and I reckon you work dodgers will have the whole she-bang traded off for whiskey before the year is out."

He whirled his horse and headed down the slope, his three companions clashing after him.

9

THE LOVELY blue dusk was sifting down from the hills like impalpable dust when Hatfield and his companions finally worked back to the Smugglers' Trail, descended into the gorge of the Rio Grande and forded the River. They rode for a mile or so farther and made a fireless camp in the shelter of an overhanging cliff.

"We'll pull in our belts tonight," Hatfield decided. "Don't want to take chances of somebody coming along and spotting us. I've got coffee and some bacon in my saddlebags, and mebbe we can knock over a couple of blue grouse in the morning. As soon as it gets light, we'll move back into the hills a piece and make a breakfast camp. Then we'll lay low till afternoon and figger on hitting Rosita after dark. I figger that's our best plan. Nobody will pay much attention to four jiggers slipping into town in the nighttime."

"Okay by me," grunted Klingman. "I've had enough fire of late to do me for a spell, anyhow. Seems that's all I been doin' durin' the past month—dodgin' smoke and fire. And I reckon that goes for you, too, Hatfield. Yuh've shore had a hot time since yuh hit this section."

"A mite too hot to be comfortable," Hatfield admitted. "I've a notion that herd will be held somewhere near Rosita," he added contemplatively, "with not more than three or four men in charge of it. The outfit would split up once they crossed the River, most of them heading back north, the chances are. If we can just find out where the herd is being held, mebbe we can land on them before they realize what is happening. I figger it's worth taking a chance on."

It was full dark the following night when the little troop rode into the sprawling Mexican village of Rosita. As they walked their horses through the straggling outskirts, Hatfield glanced about with the air of a man familiar with his surroundings. He turned down a quiet side street and, a little later, drew rein in front of a fairly large and dimly lighted *cantina*.

"Hitch the horses at the rack," he directed his companions.

They entered the *cantina* warily, glancing keenly about.

"Take a table over there in the corner, and keep your hats pulled down," Hatfield ordered in low tones.

He himself moved toward the far end of the bar, to where a smiling, round-faced Mexican stood near the till. He looked up quickly as Hatfield approached, peered with outthrust neck, an expression of utmost surprise, followed by one of pleasure, crossing his face.

"*Capitan!*" he exclaimed, hurrying forward with outstretched hand. "*Capitan!* This is indeed a glad sight for my eyes. Welcome!"

"How are you, Miguel?" the Ranger replied, returning the other's hand clasp.

"I am well, and prosperous, *Capitan*, and yourself?" said the *cantina* owner.

"Fair to middlin'," Hatfield answered.

The fat Miguel glanced about.

"What brings you here, *Capitan?*" he asked in low tones. "All know *El Lobo Solo* rides not without a purpose."

"That's what I want to talk to you about, Miguel," Hatfield replied. "Any wet cows been coming across the River lately?"

The Mexican hesitated, again glanced warily about.

"I'm not here to make trouble for any folks this side the Line," Hatfield reassured him. "You know I have no official authority south of the Border. I just happen to have a personal interest in a herd I have reason to believe landed hereabouts yesterday."

Miguel nodded. "A large herd was driven south yesterday," he admitted. "It is held in a canyon a few miles to the east, by four men from north of the River. A fifth was dispatched south to notify a buyer, who will send men to take it over and dispose of the cattle. They should arrive here sometime during the night."

Hatfield uttered an exclamation of satisfaction. "And you can tell me how to reach that canyon?"

"I will do more, *Capitan*," Miguel replied vigorously. "I, Miguel, will guide you there. Miguel does not forget the past, and it will be small repayment for a life saved at the risk of your own."

"You'll be taking a chance, if that outfit ever finds out," Hatfield warned.

The Mexican's face hardened, his black eyes glittered.

"Miguel is not a stranger to taking the chance, as doubtless you will recall, *Capitan*. I grow fat and soft in this easy life, but the heart within me still beats strong."

Hatfield chuckled.

"Yes, I remember," he admitted. "You *were* considerable of a rip-snorter when you rode with *El Zopilote*."

"Ah, The Buzzard!" Miguel translated. "He was a great *bandido, Capitan*, though so very wicked. A pity you had to shoot him. It was his boast that no man south of the River, or north of it, for that matter, could draw and shoot the gun so fast and straight as he. *Ai*, he was wrong!"

The Mexican eyed his companion a moment, glanced furtively about.

"*Capitan,*" he said in even lower tones. "I am surprised to learn you seek the cattle. I had thought—that you rode here on another matter."

Hatfield cast him a quick look.

"What matter?" he asked softly.

Again Miguel hesitated, glancing about. Then, apparently, he made up his mind to speak freely,

"Strange things are happening, *Capitan,*" he said. "There are strange stories whispered along the Border. Stories of a great leader who comes to free the people, one descended from the great ones of the days of old. Even, it is said, one reborn—the great Conqueror come again to make *Mejico* great. *El Libertador!*"

"The Liberator," Hatfield translated. "You mean somebody aims to kick up a revolution, Miguel?"

"*Si,*" Miguel replied. "So the whispers say. Already men are arming, and, I am told, drilling the drill of arms. They but wait till the gathering force is great enough. Then they will strike at the power of *El Presidente,* the oppressor."

Hatfield's eyes looked into the distance.

"A revolution, of the right sort, with the right men heading it, might not be such a bad thing down here," he said. "And some day it will come. But not the sort of hell raisin' those sidewinders would kick up. All they're out for is to set the Border country by the ears and then sneak in and skim off the cream. They're out for themselves and nobody else. What they'd start would mean only blood and tears for the folks down here, and north of the River, too. So that's it! The great *Conquistadore* himself come back to life! Of all the loco schemes! But not so loco where ignorant and superstitious folks are concerned. There are plenty who would accept the hellion, and believe in him. It might work, but not to any good end. So that's why they're smuggling stuff across the River and trading it for brand new rifles of the best make? No wonder the customs folks couldn't trace any returning goods coming down here!"

He turned suddenly to Miguel.

"The drilling and arming isn't taking place down here?"

"No," the Mexican replied. "*El Presidente's rurales* are watchful. The place of meeting is somewhere north of the River."

"On Texas soil," Hatfield nodded, "and I've a sort of hazy notion where," he added with satisfaction. "I figgered as much. The rifles and the ammunition are staying north of the River—nothing coming down here. And the smuggling bunch working robbery and widelooping as side lines on their own. Wonder what Captain Ben Wallace will say when he learns the kind of business he has been mixed up in—indirectly. Once a filibuster, always a filibuster, I reckon. He's of the breed of William Walker, the gray-eyed man of Destiny, and Crabbe, and Houston, and the others. Dream great dreams, gaze on splendid futures, and fail to see the evil going on under their very eyes!

"You did your people a good turn today, Miguel," he said to the little *cantina* owner, "an almighty good turn."

The Mexican smiled sadly. He glanced up at the tall, stern-faced Ranger.

"Ah, *Capitan*," he said wistfully, "if only *you* would lead the people. Then indeed would justice and liberty come."

But Jim Hatfield, gazing with prophetic eyes into the future, slowly shook his black head.

"The man will come in the fullness of time," he replied. "Believe—and await his coming."

Hatfield and his companions enjoyed a good meal. While they ate, Miguel vanished from his place at the end of the bar. After a leisurely cigarette, they left the *cantina* as unobtrusively as they had entered. As they approached the hitch rack, a lone horseman loomed in the darkness. It was Miguel, muffled in a *serape*, his sombrero drawn low. At a good pace he led them out of town along the trail by which they had entered. Shortly, however, he turned onto another track that veered to the east. And as they rode, Miguel and Hatfield talked earnestly in fluent Spanish, which the others could not follow.

"I'm piecing the whole thing together, now," Hatfield said at length. "The hellion took Captain Ben Wallace in proper, through his resemblance to the Conqueror. Old Ben, the dreamer, sees things as he would like them to be, so it wasn't strange he thought he saw opportunity in that jigger. He built up the smuggling business, arranged the trading of the contraband goods for rifles, justifying what he was doing by telling himself it was to a good end. And the organization he built up has run hog wild and is going in for every sort of hellishness."

"*Si, Capitan,*" agreed Miguel, "that is the situation as it stands."

"And it's due for a fall," Hatfield promised grimly.

Through the faint starlight they rode on between lofty hills until a dark canyon mouth yawned before them.

"If those hellions hear us comin', we're liable to get a hot reception," remarked Klingman.

"We'll let them hear us," Hatfield replied. "Mighty little chance to slip up on them. They'll be on the lookout. Take it easy, and act like we belonged here."

Riding at a regular pace, conversing loudly among themselves, they entered the canyon mouth. To their ears came the occasional bawling of cattle. Abruptly, forms loomed in the dark.

"That you, Carlos?" a gruff voice called in halting Spanish.

"*Si*, it is those expected," Hatfield returned easily, in the same language.

An unintelligible grunt of relief answered him. Hand close to his gun butt, he rode forward. Four men on horseback rode to meet him. Suddenly one uttered a startled exclamation.

"Hey," he barked in English, "you ain't Carlos! What the—"

Hatfield's voice blared forth, edged with steel—

"Elevate! You're covered!"

The man gave a yelp of alarm, and went for his gun; but Hatfield drew and shot him before he could clear leather. He spun from the saddle and thudded to the ground. Instantly his companions were cursing and shooting. The guns of Klingman and the two cowboys blazed fire.

In ten seconds it was all over. Clem Shore, swearing steadily, was swabbing at a gashed cheek. Beak Prescott was fumbling a handkerchief around a furrowed upper arm. Four riderless horses were fleeing in snorting flight up the canyon. Their riders lay sprawled on the ground.

"The cattle, *Capitan*," Miguel urged. "Start them moving quickly. Those who come for them may arrive at any moment, and they are many. You have little time to reach the River, and safety."

The cowmen took the hint. At top speed they got the big herd moving, pushing it as fast as possible along the track to the Smugglers' Trail, which they reached without interruption. There they said goodbye to Miguel, who shook hands all around and then faded into the darkness.

"Shove 'em," Hatfield ordered. "If that bunch coming to get them manages to figger out what's happened, we may have trouble a-plenty on our hands before we're back in Texas."

Dawn was streaking the sky when, far ahead, appeared the bluffs that banked the River. Hatfield, continually glancing back over his shoulder, uttered an exclamation. Over the crest of a rise, several miles to the rear, were pouring nearly a dozen horsemen.

"Here they come!" he shouted to the others. "Shove the critters. It's going to be a close race."

As quickly as possible they drove the weary, protesting cows, but not fast enough. The pursuit gained rapidly. Slugs began to sing overhead. To their ears came faintly the yells of the vengeful owlhoots.

"Mexicans, most of 'em," grunted Klingman. "Thank blazes for that. Oilers are seldom good shots."

"One jigger is pretty good," Hatfield returned grimly, instinctively ducking his head as a bullet whined by close. He glanced at the looming bluffs, and the broad River. They were still some distance away.

"Keep 'em moving, and right into the water," he ordered, and pulled Goldy to a halt. Backing the sorrel into the brush that lined the trail, he swung to the ground and slid his Winchester from the boot. Crouching low, he lined sights with the speeding pursuers. The rifle cracked. The distant riders ducked wildly, and yelled curses. Hatfield shifted his sights the merest trifle and again pulled trigger.

One of the riders whirled from his saddle as if plucked by a giant hand. Hatfield fired again, and emptied another saddle. The remaining horsemen jerked their mounts to a halt, then streaked them into the brush. Hatfield also backed into the shelter of the growth and shifted his position. Bullets began flicking twigs and leaves to the ground. Some came altogether too close for comfort. He shifted again, sidling Goldy along with him. His eyes never left the trail behind. He sensed movement in the chaparral some distance from where the owlhoots had taken shelter. Instantly he fired at the movement. A yell echoed the shot, and a shower of bullets.

"Sneakin' along through the brush," he muttered as he continued to move stealthily in the direction of the River. A glance in that direction showed the herd taking the water at the ford, Klingman and the cowboys urging them along. Bullets continued to clip twigs over Hatfield's head, despite his continued shifting of position. He risked another glance toward the River. The cows were streaming up the far bank. He forked the sorrel, swerved him out of the growth. His voice blared forth—

"Trail, Goldy! Trail!"

Instantly the great sorrel extended himself. Amid a storm of passing slugs he shot along the trail. One burned a streak along Hatfield's bronzed cheek. Another plucked urgently at his sleeve. Behind him sounded a wild yelling, the crackle of shots and a pounding of hoofs on the trail. But swiftly the sorrel drew away from the pursuit. Down the steep track to the water's edge he plunged without slacking speed, hit the water in a shower of spray. The shallows boiled as he surged for the far bank, onto which Klingman and the cowboys were clambering. Before he was halfway across, Hatfield heard the yells of the pursuers as they topped the steep bank. Bullets spatted against the water nearby.

But answering shots came from the far bank of the River. Old Cas Klingman and his two hands were lining sights with the owlhoots standing up against the sky. Hatfield suddenly realized that no more slugs were coming toward him.

"Reckon the boys made it a mile too hot for them," he chuckled as Goldy splashed the shallows and, a moment later, drew out upon the north bank.

Under cover of the rifles of his companions, Hatfield made his way to the top of the bank. A few moments

more and they were shoving the herd across Texas soil.
A few wild bullets speeded them upon their way; but the
pursuit did not attempt to ford the River.

Through the scorched and blackened defile they
pushed the herd, and out onto the desert, above which
now the sky was deep blue, the air crystal clear. The
Haunted Hills loomed mistily in the east, with no ghostly
banners streaming from their summits. As sunset was
blazing scarlet and gold in the west and the crags were
tipped with saffron flame, they halted the worn and
weary cattle within sight of the incompleted Tumbling
K ranchhouse.

"I'm takin' no more chances," Klingman declared
grimly. "I'm puttin' every hand I have on guard tonight
and until we get ready to head for Como."

The Tumbling K cowboys came streaming out to meet
them, whooping with excitement and yelling congratula-
tions.

"Figger yuh'd be disappointed," grunted Klingman,
frowning blackly to conceal his pleasure at the warmth
of the greeting. "Just think of all the red-eye yuh'd have
been able to buy if I hadn't showed up again!"

10

~~~~~~~~~~~

BERT PIERCE informed them that the sheriff and his posse never got beyond the northern edge of the desert.

"It stormed all day," he explained, "and White didn't dare take a chance. They found old Andy Cahil knocked on the head and tied up in his cabin. He'll pull through, all right. Doc McChesney did a good job on him. He was out bangin' a tin tub all day today, tryin' to get his maverickin' bees back home. He's madder'n any bee in the lot."

After allowing the cows to rest for several days, the cutting-out job was finished and the Tumbling K shipping herd readied for the trail. It rolled northward early in the morning with the whole outfit, and some borrowed hands, in attendance, for Klingman still was taking no chances.

Armed and vigilant point or lead men rode near the head of the marching herd. A third of the way back rode equally armed and vigilant swing riders, where the herd would begin to bend at a change of direction. Another third of the way back were the flank riders, whose nom inal duty, assisted by the swing riders, was to block their own cattle from wandering sideways, and also to drive off any foreign cattle that might try to join the herd. The force of point, swing and flank riders was double the number usually used for a herd of this size. Also, much more numerous than usual were the drag riders who brought up the rear. The chuck wagon, containing men armed with rifles followed close behind.

In addition, Hatfield assigned two men on each side of the moving herd to act as outriders. They flanked the herd about a mile distant on either side, keeping a sharp lookout for anything that might appear off-color.

Hatfield himself, and Klingman, rode some distance in front of the herd, alert for anything suspicious.

"If things get worse, we'll have to call on a company of United States Cavalry to run a herd to town," the rancher growled disgustedly. "Or anyhow, a couple of Rangers," he added.

They reached Como at sunset and delivered the cows safely to the shipping pens. The whole outfit breathed a sigh of relief.

As Hatfield and Klingman sat eating their supper in the Alhambra saloon, *Don* Ramon Garcia came through the swinging doors and glanced keenly about. His eyes gleamed as they rested on the Ranger. However, with a short nod, he passed to the bar without pausing at their table. Hatfield noted that he was dusty and travel stained and looked in need of sleep.

"Ain't we never goin' to be in the clear from that blasted oiler?" Cas Klingman growled. "Everywhere we go he shows up. I wonder what's due to bust loose now?"

Hatfield smiled slightly, an amused gleam in his green eyes, but said nothing.

Klingman got paid for his cows the following morning, and immediately banked the money.

"The price of a plug of eatin' tobacco is all I'm packin', or keepin' in the house, from now on," he said.

Evening of the following day found them back at the Tumbling K ranchhouse, work upon which was to be resumed the next morning.

In Cibolero, Sheriff White had greeted Hatfield with enthusiasm.

"A fine chore yuh did, son," he applauded. "I still think yuh should be a peace officer. Come in soon and have a talk with me."

"I'll be in very soon to have a talk with you," Hatfield promised, with a meaning that was lost on the sheriff.

Soon after supper, Cas Klingman was snoring on his bunk in the barn. Jim Hatfield also went to bed, but not to sleep. When he was sure Klingman was safe in the land of dreams, he rose softly, dressed, and led Goldy from the barn. He mounted the sorrel and rode swiftly along the track that led to the Cibolero Trail. At the forks, where what was left of Andy Cahil's bee ranch reposed in peace, he turned south.

Swiftly he rode, until he struck the desert. Then he turned west and skirted the hills until he reached the mouth of the gloomy canyon where sat the cabin in which he had been imprisoned. He proceeded up the gorge with great caution, pausing from time to time to listen. But the canyon remained utterly silent, and apparently deserted. Dawn was streaking the sky when he passed the lonely, silent cabin, giving it a wide berth, although he was confident the owlhoots would no longer take a chance by occupying it. He regained the trail and was greatly pleased to note signs of the recent passage of horses. Now he rode with even greater caution, pausing on the crest of each rise to search carefully the terrain beyond. He was some miles beyond the cabin when he smelled a faint tang of wood smoke filtering through the clean air of morning. He pulled up and sat listening for some time.

Still the canyon remained silent. It had narrowed somewhat and the dark walls seemed even taller. So close together was their overhang that although morning was well advanced, the depths were still shadowy. He waited a little longer, then sent Goldy forward at a slow pace.

Another half mile and the canyon opened out somewhat, the growth that choked it thinned a bit. But at about half the distance to the box wall the cliffs abruptly drew together to form a narrow gut considerably less than half the width of the gorge below the inward bulge. Hatfield had a premonition that beyond the bulge was what he sought. For some moments he debated his further procedure. Finally he sidled Goldy into the brush, left him tied in a small clearing completely inclosed by growth and proceeded on foot.

As he drew near the bulge, he saw that the stone protuberance that formed it did not extend to the cliff tops, but was less than a hundred feet high.

He saw more. Zigzagging up the barrier was a ledge that wound to its top. Moving with the utmost care he reached the foot of the ledge. Again he paused, an idea growing in his mind.

"If I can sneak up that shelf to the top of the bulge, I've a notion I can see what's going on around the bend," he told himself, adding grimly, "and if I happen to get spotted while I'm doing it, I'll have a good chance of coming down like a plugged squirrel from a tree top."

For some minutes he stood listening, but heard nothing. The smell of wood smoke persisted, however, and he was convinced he was not far from the secret hangout of the owlhoot band.

"Well, here goes," he muttered, and began climbing the ledge.

It was quite narrow at first, but as he proceeded up the beetling wall of rock, it widened. Also, it sloped inward, like the petal of a flower. Soon he found himself in a sort of narrow rock lane and out of sight of anybody who might approach by way of the canyon floor below. Another few minutes and he reached the rough and broken crest of the bulge, which proved to be at least three hundred yards in width. Confident that he was still invisible from below, he crept across it. He had covered perhaps two-thirds of the distance when he heard a murmur of voices somewhere ahead.

With the greatest caution he stole on, pausing from time to time to listen. As he advanced the sound of the voices grew louder, accompanied by a muffled thumping. He covered the last fifty yards flat on his stomach and crawling painfully over the broken surface of the stone, the sun beating down on his exposed back with furnace heat. At last he reached the ragged lip of the precipice and peered over. His lips pursed in a soundless whistle.

Between the bulge and the end wall of the canyon, which was now no great distance away, was a wide amphitheatre, roughly circular in shape. Along the side wall were a number of flimsily built brush and pole lean-tos, before some of which burned cooking fires. Fronting the open faced huts was an open space of dusty naked rock, upon which the rays of the sun beat fiercely. And marching back and forth across the open space were some two hundred ragged, bare-foot straw-sombreroed Mexican peons. Over each man's shoulder slanted a new and gleaming rifle.

In slovenly military formation they marched and counter-marched. Forming lines of squads, of twos, wheeling, reversing, turning to a ragged company line. Barking orders at them in illiterate Spanish was a tall, evil-faced Mexican who wore a sword strapped to his waist. He cursed and reviled his shambling charges.

"Look sharp, *cabrons!*" he barked. "Tomorrow *El Libertador* himself reviews you. He must have pride in his Army of Liberation!"

But to Jim Hatfield, the weary, barefoots slouching in the hot sun did not look like men expecting liberation.

They had more of the look of scourged slaves. He noted that lounging comfortably in the shade of the cliff were nearly a dozen armed men who kept watching eyes on the marching "soldiers."

Hatfield's gaze rested on the rifles the marchers bore.

"Good guns, all right," he muttered, "but I'd be willing to bet a hatful of pesos they aren't loaded, and those poor devils don't get a chance to get their hands on any ammunition, either. But just tho oame there's the making of plenty of trouble here."

Wary lest one of the lounging guards might chance to glance upward and spot him, even in his concealment behind the jagged rim, he slid back from the edge, considered a moment and then crept across the parapet to the side that faced the west wall of the canyon. He peered over cautiously.

The trail ran along the base of the bulge and he quickly decided that the approach was invisible to those within the amphitheatre.

"They can't see anybody until he's right around the cliff," he told himself. "This thing is made to order, proving there are no slips and there isn't a guard posted outside. There isn't now, that's certain, and the chances are there isn't one at any time. The hellions feel pretty safe up here, I reckon."

He studied the terrain for another few minutes, noting that the thick chaparral grew to within a few yards of the trail. Then he turned and made his way to the ledge. He descended rapidly, paused at the base of the cliff for a moment to listen and slipped into the brush. Without mishap he made his way back to his waiting horse, mounted and rode down the canyon.

He rode swiftly, but cautiously, keeping as much as possible in the shadow of the growth that flanked the trail, pausing at the crest of each rise to study the ground ahead.

He had covered perhaps half the distance to the cabin when, on pausing on the crest of a sag, he saw a man riding toward him, up-canyon. A man who rode furtively, studying the growth on either side, examining the surface of the trail, pausing from time to time to peer and listen.

Hatfield backed Goldy into the fringe of the growth and watched the man's approach. Suddenly he chuckled softly. In the broad-shouldered, rugged figure he recognized *Don* Ramon Garcia.

"That jigger isn't doing so bad, after all," he told himself. "My hunch concerning him was a straight one, all right. Is *he* going to be surprised!"

He backed the sorrel still deeper into the chaparral, until both horse and rider were completely concealed from the trail. Peering through the fringe of branches, he waited.

Finally to his ears came the click of approaching hoofs. He saw Garcia loom over the lip of the sag, pause to glance keenly about, then, apparently satisfied, ride slowly forward. Hatfield waited until he was past his hiding place then called out, a note of laughter in his voice—

"You're on the right track, all right, Garcia!"

11

D_ON RAMON_ whirled in his saddle at the sound of Hatfield's voice, hand streaking to his gun. He stared, his jaw dropping as Hatfield rode from the brush and looked him up and down with mirthful eyes.

"How's things down to the Customs Office?" Hatfield asked in conversational tones.

Garcia's grip tightened on his gun butt; then abruptly his hand dropped. He straightened in his saddle, whirled his mount.

"*Sangre de Dios!* I know you!" he whooped. "I've got you placed at last! You are Captain McDowell's *Teniente* —Lieutenant! You're the Lone Wolf!"

"Been called that," Hatfield admitted, his smile broadening. "How come you to be up this canyon?"

Don Ramon flushed slightly and he looked embarrassed.

"I trailed you here," he admitted. "I lost you when you entered the canyon. For a long time I waited outside that cabin down the trail. Finally I crept up to it and found it empty. Then I rode on. I've been keeping a close watch on you ever since you showed up in this section. You had me badly puzzled. At first I thought you to be the leader of the smugglers. Later I didn't know what to think. I've been working on this case for six months, and getting exactly nowhere."

Hatfield chuckled. "Looks like we were trailing each other for a spell," he replied. "I couldn't figger you out for a while. Had some sort of the same notion about you as you had about me. Then I started putting things together and figgered out the answer. I knew, of course, that the Customs Office had somebody working in this section, perhaps more than one. Nobody else fitted in. Come on, now, let's be getting out of this crack. There are a few jiggers up the canyon who might take a notion to ride this way. If they spot us here, a little scheme I've figgered out won't work."

Together the Ranger and the Customs Officer rode down the canyon. Hatfield acquainted Garcia with what he found at the head of the canyon, and outlined the plan he had formulated.

"It should work," agreed *Don* Ramon. "With luck, we should capture the whole outfit."

"Anyhow, I figger we'll bag the big he-wolf of the pack, and that's the important thing," Hatfield promised grimly.

Night had fallen when they drew rein in front of the sheriff's office in Cibolero. They paused for a moment outside, Hatfield fumbling with the concealed pocket in his belt, Garcia fishing something from inside his shirt. Together they entered the lighted office, where Sheriff White sat at his desk.

The sheriff stared, his jaw dropping, his eyes bulging. On Hatfield's breast gleamed the silver star of the Texas Rangers. *Don* Ramon wore the badge of a Customs Inspector.

"For Pete's sake!" gasped the sheriff, when he could find his voice. "Are you hellions goin' to a masquerade dance or somethin'?"

Hatfield chuckled, his green eyes sunny.

"Captain McDowell asked me to remind you that you

still owe him five dollars from that poker game up at the XT spread twenty years ago," he said.

Sheriff White leaped to his feet. "Why, that ornery old pelican!" he yelped. "That game was as crooked as a barrel of snakes! Why, one hand he showed up with four aces against my four kings, and I'd been plumb careful to deal him four queens! Say—you *must* be a Ranger, if Bill McDowell told yuh about that game!"

"Yes," remarked Garcia, "and—the *Lone Wolf!* Ever hear of *him?*"

The sheriff had. He stared, almost in awe, at the legendary figure whose exploits were the talk of the whole Southwest.

"The Lone Wolf!" he repeated. "Yes, I've heard of him. I might have knowed it. You do things like him, but yuh don't look just like what I'd figgered the Lone Wolf to be. Folks always said he was a big ice-eyed jigger who never smiled, and it 'pears to me *you're* laughin' about half the time."

"Perhaps those gentlemen saw him behind a gun barrel," Garcia observed dryly. "I've a notion that would make somewhat of a difference."

"And Garcia a Customs man!" he marvelled. "Well, if this don't take the hide off the bull!"

Hatfield proceeded to give White the lowdown on the situation.

"Get your deputies together and be ready to ride at midnight," he directed. "Only the deputies. Don't take a chance on a posse. That might tip the sidewinders off. Send one deputy to the Tumbling K ranchhouse right away. Tell Klingman to have his boys at Andy Cahil's bee ranch, at the forks, waiting for us. That'll give us all the posse we'll need. Cas and the boys will be plumb pleased to get in a few licks against that outfit, and I figger they'd ought to have the chance. I've had them along with me and know they're to be depended on.

"By starting from here at midnight, I figger we will give *El Libertador* and his bunch plenty of time to make the head of the canyon before we get there. Don't want to have any late arrivals coming up behind us at the wrong time. It's a salty outfit with a bad hombre at the head of it. I figger they won't give up without a fight."

"What about them soldier jiggers yuh spoke about?" asked the sheriff. "If the whole two hundred land on us, we'll have about as much chance as a rabbit in a houndawg's mouth."

"They won't," Hatfield assured him. "The poor devils will be glad of a chance to get out of the mess they've been roped into, and besides, they are not armed, except with empty rifles. Nothing to worry about from them. Now I figger to have a bite of chuck and then a couple of hours of shut-eye. Garcia and I will be ready to ride when you are."

Hatfield and Garcia ate in the Busted Flush, at separate tables. The Ranger noted that Steve Tule was not present at his usual place at the end of the bar. As he ate, he pondered the ranch and saloon owner's rather unusual name.

"Stephen—*Estaban*," he mused. "And Tules was what the Aztecs called the Spaniards when they first arrived in Mexico. "*Estaban Tule,* which translates in English as Stephen the Spaniard. Fits, all right. Well, I hope to learn more about that before many hours have passed."

In company with Sheriff White and his three deputies, he and Garcia left the darkened town at midnight. They rode south at a swift pace until they reached Andy Cahil's bee ranch, where they found Cas Klingman and the Tumbling K hands eagerly awaiting them. Sheriff White swore in the outfit as deputies.

Pausing just long enough for a cup of steaming coffee with old Andy, they hit the trail once more. It was dull daylight when, after skirting the foothills, they reached the canyon mouth. They proceeded up the gorge with the greatest caution. The last half mile to the bulge they moved on foot, stealing noiselessly through the brush, having left their horses in the little clearing that accommodated Goldy the day before. Near where the trail curved around the bulge to reach the amphitheatre they paused, lying securely hidden in the chaparral.

For some time Hatfield watched the deserted trail.

" 'Pears like they're all in there, but I want to be sure," he told his companions. "I'm going to have a look-see."

He stole from the brush and began climbing the ledge up the face of the cliff. He reached the jagged summit of the bulge and stole across it until he could peer cautiously down into the rock walled amphitheatre. For a moment he gazed, his eyes glowing, then he turned and quickly made his way back to the waiting posse.

"Everything set," he told them. "The soldiers are lined up against the side cliff, in company formation. *El Libertador* and his bunch are grouped in front of them, their backs to the trail. *El Libertador* is haranguing his army. We should be able to catch them settin'. Let's go."

With Hatfield and Sheriff White leading, the posse slid out of the brush. They swerved swiftly around the curve of the bulge and were inside the amphitheatre before the owlhoots realized what was going on. Hatfield's voice rang out—

"In the name of the State of Texas! Steve Tule, and others, I arrèst you for robbery and murder. Anything you say may be used against you."

For a moment it looked like the surprise was complete, that the capture would be made without firing a shot. The owlhoots, "caught settin'," and covered by a score of guns, didn't have a chance. Resistance would be tantamount to suicide. Steve Tule, his face ashen, his eyes wild, glared at Hatfield, but dared not make a move.

And then the unexpected happened, something that

not even Jim Hatfield had counted on. The *peon* "soldiers" did not understand what was said, but they saw the Ranger's gleaming star, and the badges on the breasts of his companions. One gave a yell of terror, threw down his empty gun and bolted for the open canyon, chattering a string of incoherent Spanish.

One and all, his companions followed his example. Instantly a solid mass of fear-frantic humanity interposed between the posse and the grouped owlhoots.

The owlhoots, with the courage of desperation, seized the chance handed them. They scattered in all directions; guns out and blazing. The walls of the amphitheatre seemed to reel and rock to the roar of sixshooters.

Fired with the courage of despair, the outlaws fought like cornered rats. Dodging in and out among the fleeing *peons,* they afforded difficult targets. Quickly two of White's deputies were down, one with a smashed shoulder, the other with a bullet hole through his thigh. The Mexican drill master, Sancho, his gun empty, rushed at Hatfield with a long knife. The Ranger shot him so close that the flame of his Colt scorched his swarthy skin. Two of the Tumbling K punchers received flesh wounds but continued to pull trigger. A moment later, Jim Hatfield lowered his smoking guns and gazed on the bloody scene. All but three of the smugglers were dead, and these three were wounded. Sheriff White holstered his guns and hurried forward to secure his prisoners.

Bert Pierce was dancing about, spewing curses.

"Right where I got that load of bird shot from old Andy!" he wailed. "A whole hunk of meat knocked loose! Ain't I ever goin' to be able to set down in comfort!"

Hatfield was peering into the faces of the dead men.

"Tule!" he exclaimed. "The hellion isn't here!"

"I saw him slide around the bulge toward the trail, while the shootin' was goin' strong," gasped one of the wounded deputies.

Hatfield raced around the bulge. Far down the trail a figure was fleeing. Hatfield sped in pursuit. A moment later Tule dived into the brush and vanished. Hatfield redoubled his efforts, but before he could reach the spot, Tule reappeared, mounted on a tall black horse, and thundered off down the trail.

At top speed, Hatfield raced to where he had left Goldy. He mounted the sorrel and sent him crashing through the brush to the trail. Tule had a long lead, but Hatfield had confidence in Goldy's speed and endurance. He settled himself in the saddle and urged the sorrel to his utmost efforts.

He topped the rise, saw Tule, far ahead, driving his horse to the limit of its endurance. He vanished over a distant crest. Hatfield talked to the sorrel, encouraging him with word and hand. Goldy gave all that was in him. His powerful legs shot backward like steel pistons, his irons beat the trail with a drumroll of sound. He snorted, slugged his head above the bit, and literally poured his long body over the ground.

Another rise, and again Hatfield spotted his quarry, nearer now. The tall black was a superb animal, but he had more than met his match in Goldy. Another long slope, Goldy flashing down the opposite side of the sag, and Hatfield drew his Winchester from the boot. Tule was now within long rifle range.

Steadying the sorrel, Hatfield flung the rifle to his shoulder. His eyes glanced along the sights. The rifle spurted smoke, and he saw Tule duck. Shot after shot he fired, kicking up dust at the black's feet, causing Tule to bend low over his flying mount's neck. And then a bend in the trail hid him from view. Hatfield slid the rifle back into the boot and gave all his attention to riding. At a dead run Goldy took the bend around which Tule had vanished. As the trail straightened out again, Hatfield

jerked him to a sliding, slithering halt. Less than a score
of yards distant, Tule sat his blowing horse, his gun out
and ready. The black muzzle lined with Hatfield's breast.

Even as Tule pulled trigger, Hatfield hurled himself
sideways from the saddle. He heard the roar of Tule's
gun, and the whine of the passing slug. Prone on the
ground, he jerked his own Colt and answered the outlaw
leader shot for shot.

A bullet nicked his shoulder. Another fanned his face
with the wind of its passing. A third ripped his sleeve
from wrist to elbow, leaving a stinging welt in its wake.
Then he gazed through the smoke of his guns at Tule's
tall form outlined against the sky, reeling in the saddle
of his rearing horse.

He fell slowly, sliding from the hull, his gun dropping
from his nerveless hand. He hit the trail with a thud and
lay sprawling and motionless.

Hatfield got stiffly to his feet, walked forward and
gazed down into the distorted face of the dead outlaw.
Between Tule's glazing eyes was a black bullet hole.

"Got him dead center," Hatfield muttered. "Well, I
reckon that's about all."

After a long look at the slain owlhoot, he mounted and
rode back to the amphitheatre at the head of the canyon.
He found Sheriff White and Klingman finishing the chore
of patching up the wounded, none of whom were dan-
gerously hurt.

"The 'soldiers' are all holed up in the brush somewhere," White told him. "What will we do about 'em?"

"Forget them," Hatfield replied. "They'll make their
way back to Mexico and glad of the chance. I've a notion
they're pretty well fed up on revolutions. You can send
a couple of carts down here to pack the rifles back to
town. You won't need to buy any guns for quite a spell."

There was an ample supply of provisions in the lean-

tos. The possemen decided to cook a much needed meal
before heading back to town. As they ate, Bert Pierce
standing up, Hatfield talked with White and Klingman.

"It was a funny set-up," he observed. "You'll recollect,
Cas, I had a long pow-wow with Miguel, the *cantina*
owner, as he rode out of Rosita. Miguel was able to tell
me enough to make it possible for me to pretty well piece
the picture together. It seems Ben Wallace met Tule in
Mexico City. He was struck by Tule's remarkable resemblance to Hernán Cortes, the Spanish Conqueror of the
Aztecs. Obsessed with his dreams of a Mexican empire,
Wallace thought he saw opportunity in Tule. He per-
suaded him to accept the part of *Libertador* and field
leader of the revolution. I reckon Tule saw opportunity
in Wallace. Anyhow, he pretended to fall in with his
plans. He told Wallace he actually was a descendant of
Cortes and his Aztec sweetheart, the Lady Marina.
Mebbe he was. He had a Spanish look about him, though
he talked more like a New Englander than anything else.

"Wallace needed money to buy arms and outfit his
army of liberation. He worked up the smuggling scheme
to get it. Smuggling is looked upon rather lightly down
here, as you all know. If you can get by with it, nobody
thinks any the less of you. Captain Ben felt he was justified in a little mild law breaking. He had connections and
was able to trade the contraband for the rifles and other
things he needed. He brought Tule back to Texas with
him and set him up in business. With Tule's help, he got
together a prime outfit of hellions and set them to work.
That's when Tule began to take over on his own hook. He
pulled the wool over Captain Ben's eyes for fair. While
attending to the smuggling, as he was supposed to, he
branched out into robbery and widelooping. He led Wallace to believe that an owlhoot outfit was working in the
section. Captain Ben never realized that it was his own
'patriots' who were responsible for the hellraising going

on in the section. I'm confident he would never have
stood for it."

"That's right," agreed the sheriff. "Old Ben isn't the sort
to go in for robbery and murder, no matter how loco he
is. How did yuh get a line on Tule, Jim?"

Hatfield paused to pour a cup of coffee.

"I never did get a real line on him until after my talk
with Miguel," he replied, although I'd been wondering
about him for quite a while. You see, I figgered Tule was
lying to folks about where he came from. He claimed to
be a Kentuckian, but I don't figger anybody ever heard
a Kentuckian use expressions like, 'I want to know!'
'Callate,' and so on. Those are Down East colloquialisms.
And I've observed that when a jigger tries to cover up
where he really came from, he'll bear watching. But for
quite a spell it was Garcia here who had me guessing,
especially after I discovered those rifles in the hut and
got to wondering what they were to be used for. Garcia
shows his Spanish blood, and admits it. He's the sort of
jigger meant to be a leader. It sure looked to me for a
while like Garcia was the head of the outfit. But he didn't
measure up right. He was too open-and-above-board.
Then he was always around when things happened,
which certainly wouldn't be the case with a jigger who
needed to keep in the clear. It began to look to me like
Garcia was mighty busy trying to find out what was going on, and that was all. After I'd definitely decided on
Tule as the leader of the smugglers, it wasn't over hard
to figger Garcia as the Customs House man I knew must
bo working in the section."

He grinned at *Don* Ramon, and rolled a cigarette before continuing.

"Tule spotted me for a Ranger right off," he said.
"Those jiggers who dropped a loop on me when I
beached the silver boat gave it away. One piped up I
must be the jigger the big Boss had warned them against.

Then that jigger trying to knife me in the room at Brad's stable sort of cinched the matter. I knew he was part of the smuggler outfit, all right. I took a tobacco pouch full of marihuana off him, just like another one I took off the sidewinder I did for that night they locked me up in the cabin down the canyon. That's where the hellions put another one over on Captain Ben. Old Ben would never have condoned smuggling marihuana into the country. He knows what that stuff does to folks, especially to Mexicans. Dobe dollars were what Captain Ben figgered them to deal in. The silver in the dobe dollar is worth a lot more than the face value of the coin. As you all know, smugglers make a handsome profit by slipping them in and melting them down. Of course, the regular smuggling procedure is then to trade the silver for goods that can be sold at a handsome profit below the Line. But Captain Ben was trading for arms and ammunition. Which was why no return goods were showing up in Mexico, contrary to usual procedure. But nacherly the sidewinders Tule got together couldn't resist an on-the-side deal in marihuana and other stuff easy to handle and dispose of."

He paused, rolling another cigarette with the slim fingers of his left hand.

"And I reckon that's about all," he said.

"What will we do about Ben Wallace?" the sheriff asked.

"Nothing," Hatfield replied. "I'm confident he didn't have any part in anything other than the smuggling, and it would be mighty hard to get a smuggling conviction against a man of his popularity in this country. I've a notion he's had his lesson and won't make any more trouble. He'll settle down to ranching from now on, and forget about Sam Houston and his Grand Plan. Hope he lives to see the day when Mexico will be a free country, prosperous and progressive. It'll come, in time."

He glanced about, cocked an eye toward the westerly sun.

"Well, seeing that everybody has finished eating, I reckon we might as well start for town," he observed. "I want to head back to the Post tomorrow. Captain Bill will have another little chore ready for me by the time I get there. You and Garcia can finish mopping up here. Those prisoners will talk, and line you up on where to drop a loop on any of the bunch that may be still running loose. Reckon you can finish building your *casa* without my help, Cas. I've lined the boys up pretty well on what else is to be done."

Sheriff White and Klingman watched him ride away the following afternoon, tall and graceful atop his great golden horse, and watched regretfully. He rode north by east, although Ranger headquarters were at Franklin, to the west.

Before the big Barbed Five ranchhouse he pulled rein, dismounted and climbed the steps. Old Ben Wallace was seated in the big living room, staring at the portrait of Hernán Cortes, the Conqueror. He glanced up as the tall Ranger entered, complete understanding in his eyes.

"Reckon yuh've come for me," he observed.

But Jim Hatfield smiled, and shook his head.

"No, Captain Ben," he replied. "You have broken your country's laws, but I guess you felt justified in doing what you did. I know you would not have countenanced what Tule and his hellions pulled. I merely came to say goodbye and wish you luck. Remember what you said about great men dying too soon? Well, what has happened may help you to realize that sometimes great men live too *long*. That is, if they don't handle their greatness carefully."

"I guess that's so," Wallace admitted. He smiled, sadly, as Hatfield opened the door.

"Anyhow," he said, "it was a great dream."

Hatfield gazed down at him from his great height, compassion and understanding in his strangely colored eyes.

"Something to have dreamed," he said, as he passed out and closed the door. "Something to have dreamed!"

THE END